Return Of Secrets

Book Eight of the Vital Secrets Series

D.F. Hart

2 Of Harts Publishing

Acknowledgments

In remembrance of Joy Lee Everheart – fellow DHS alum, avid reader and gamer, and most excellent friend. You are loved and missed.

To the incomparable Carrie Wood, Alpha reader extraordinaire, whose enthusiasm and honest feedback I cherish.

To Stacy S, who backed my Kickstarter and whose experiences as a computer tech provided a superb framework on which to base primary witness Steph Bronski in this story.

Speaking of techs, this one's for you; you awesome men and women behind the scenes who wade through piles of evidence day in and day out, wielding science as your weapon of choice, to help ensure that the innocent are cleared - and that the guilty pay. I honor and thank you.

D.F.

The Vital Secrets Series

Wall of Secrets (prequel)
Book of Secrets
List of Secrets
Web of Secrets
Path of Secrets
Carnival of Secrets
House of Secrets
End of Secrets
Return of Secrets
Game of Secrets – Fall 2024
Network of Secrets – Fall 2025
War of Secrets – Fall 2026

Visit ***2ofharts.com*** to sign up for my newsletter and get both the prequel and a special bonus supplement to the series!

Follow me on:

BookBub
Facebook
Goodreads

Chapter One

"It's the third time I've worn one of these. You'd think I'd be used to it," Bella Amsel Thomas grumbled to herself as she once again adjusted her mortarboard, then took another look at her reflection.

That will have to do, I guess.

She shrugged as she tucked away the small comb she'd used to help smooth her hair around the strangely fitting cap's edges, then turned slightly to check that the orange velvet hood that designated her as a Master of Arts graduate was properly aligned.

Bella left the ladies' room and took her assigned place in the Liberal Arts queue just as the first strains of "Pomp and Circumstance" began to play.

"Ironic, isn't it?" the lady standing in line behind her said.

"What's ironic?"

"That we're in Arlington, Texas marching out to take our seats to a song originally composed in 1901 to commemorate a *British* king's coronation," the woman revealed with a smile.

"Interesting," Bella mused. "I did not know that."

"Music major," her fellow graduate said with a shrug as she

pointed out the pink honor society cords draped over her shoulders. "Just one of the many tidbits in my degree path."

"Ah. Pretty color."

"I thought so, too. What does yours stand for?"

"The red, white, and blue one is for the French honors society, and the black, gold and red one is for German."

"Where's Mommy?" Charlie asked as he fidgeted with the tiny clip-on tie at his neck.

"She will be coming out here from that doorway right over there just anytime now," Nathan murmured and pointed.

"Okay," Charlie answered, content for the moment, and Nathan smiled as he gazed around at all the other families who had gathered in the huge auditorium to witness the graduation ceremony on a warm Saturday mid-May morning.

Several minutes passed, and then Nathan was pointing.

"See? There's Mommy now," he told an excited Charlie, who immediately stood up in his chair and waved both hands to get Bella's attention.

She saw them, smiled, winked, then blew them a kiss as she made her way to her seat.

"She looks beautiful," a misty-eyed Jandy said, her face beaming with the quintessential 'proud big sister' look. "And I bet she's happy to be done with her degrees, finally."

Down the row, Nathan, Faith, and Rick all nodded their agreement.

"You know it," Nathan replied. "And, she already has four interviews lined up next week alone. Someone as fluent as she is in multiple languages is a highly desired commodity in the business world."

"I thought she wanted to teach?" Rick commented.

"That was her original intention," Nathan shared. "But we were both surprised at the level of interest she's gotten from both public and private sector, so she's decided to explore those options as well."

The traditional commencement music continued to play until at long last the final graduate was seated, and all eyes turned toward the podium, where the president of the university launched into his welcome speech.

Over in Fort Worth, a pale-faced Lizzie Zimmerman was rudely interrupted from her Saturday morning routine by yet another extreme bout of nausea. Once it had subsided again, she rinsed her mouth and spit several times, then finished wrangling the long brown hair that had only been partially restrained into a proper ponytail.

"Okay, little one," she murmured as she patted her slightly rounded stomach. "How about we humor Mommy today and at least let me keep *some* coffee down?"

Morning sickness had kicked in with a vengeance several days before, just as Lizzie passed the two-month mark of her pregnancy. It'd been particularly heartbreaking for her to realize that the life-sustaining nectar she depended on so much had firmly landed on the 'top three most nauseating things to eat or drink' list.

She made her way down the hall and through the living room to the kitchen, where Donny was putting the finishing touches on French toast and bacon. The aroma wafting to her overrode her stomach's perpetual sensation of being on an amusement park ride and made her mouth water.

"That smells really good," she said as she sniffed the air, then cast a wistful side-eyed glance at the coffeemaker on the counter that beckoned to her soul like a siren to a lonely sailor.

"Think I should try it again?"

"Your call, honey, but I think the baby's made it clear. For the time being, at least, coffee's not a good idea."

"This sucks," she grumbled, then stopped herself as her husband raised an eyebrow.

"I don't mean the baby, I just... I *need* my coffee, Donny. He or she couldn't pick anything else to deprive me of?"

"It's okay," he answered. "I know you didn't mean the baby. And I get your frustration, I really do. The good news is that according to some of the articles I've been reading, a lot of women get through the morning sickness stage by the end of the first trimester. So hopefully, this phase won't last very much longer."

Lizzie's ears perked up.

"Really? Oh, God. Here's hoping I am in that group."

Donny chuckled as she sat at the table, and he crossed the small space to set down a plate in front of her.

"Here's hoping. In the meantime, I called my mom for advice. She said ginger tea can really help."

Lizzie's nose wrinkled even as she cut into her French toast.

"That does not sound appealing in the slightest. But if it will help, then let's give it a shot."

"I was hoping to hear you say that – because I already made you some."

He went back to the counter and returned to her side with a full mug of the freshly brewed concoction and the sugar bowl. He placed them both in front of her, then sat next to her and took her hand.

She grinned.

"You keep being sweet to me and I might just have to keep you around."

Donny laughed before he leaned over and kissed her.

"And I can't imagine anyone else I'd rather be kept by. Now drink your tea."

In Irving, Annie Adams yawned, then tested the waters by gently stretching. She frowned as she reluctantly stumbled out of the comfort of her bed for the shower – and winced as her sore muscles screamed with every step.

It was worth it, she reminded herself. *I really needed my own space.*

She'd gone from staying at Lizzie and Donnie's to bunking with Grace again until she'd found a suitable apartment. And her friends had rallied around her; Friday evening had seen the four of them, and Hank, hauling her belongings to her new place - including everything she'd put into storage when Ben died. But they'd only gotten the bigger pieces of furniture put into place in the new apartment before they called it a night around one in the morning.

Annie knew all too well that the rest of her weekend would be spent unpacking boxes and setting up house, and she grimaced as she padded barefoot down the hall to the living room, where the rows of stacked boxes along the longest wall mocked her.

"I swear they multiplied overnight. And of course, the ones marked 'bathroom' are at the bottom. Figures," she grumbled on a sigh as she scanned the pile's labels.

She moved boxes out of her way until she could get to a couple of towels, then opened one of her suitcases and pulled out a t-shirt, underwear, and yoga pants. Yawning again, she made it all the way into the bathroom before she remembered that her shower curtain, bathmat, soap, and shampoo were still packed up.

Dammit. Gonna be a long, long day.

Annie dropped the towels and clothes onto the bathroom counter, then pivoted back toward the living room to grab the other items she needed. But her cell phone ringing diverted her to the kitchen where she'd plugged in the device to charge overnight.

"Good morning, tiny," she heard Hank say when she answered the phone. "Want some help today? I know there's a lot left to do. What do you say? I'll even bring breakfast."

"I'd like that – but only if you're sure you want to waste your day doing something as boring as unpacking."

"If I wasn't sure, I wouldn't have offered, tiny. See you in about a half-hour."

"Can we make it forty-five? I really need a hot shower, but I don't even have the curtain hung up yet."

"Sore, huh?"

"It feels like I've been run over by a bus."

He chuckled.

"Let's make it an hour, then."

"Thanks. See you soon."

I know just the thing, Hank thought to himself as he disconnected the call. He added socks and running shoes to his casual attire of black jogger pants and a form-fitting blue t-shirt, then grabbed his wallet and keys.

His first stop was at a big-name superstore on the way to Annie's place. Hank found what he was looking for with little difficulty, made his purchases, then swung by the donut shop to pick up a half-dozen cronuts, the delectable pastries that Annie had introduced him to.

Breakfast and gifts in hand, he started his truck and started his drive twenty minutes to the east.

As he drove, he reflected on the unexpected turn of events that had led him to Annie Adams, and he smiled at his reflection in his rearview mirror.

She'd offered unconditional comfort and support when his best friend Cruz Delgado was killed on the job back in March. And when Annie had been devastated by fellow agent and boyfriend Ben Tinsing's murder not long afterward, Hank had gladly returned the favor.

Through their common pain, they'd bonded.

Annie had literally saved his life not even two months after that, and once the threat known as Cesar Nelson had been neutralized, Hank had acted completely on impulse and shocked the hell out of both Annie and himself by kissing her.

The fact that she'd not only not stopped him, but kissed him back, had shifted his world a solid one-hundred-eighty degrees, but in a great way.

Definitely a great way, he acknowledged as he took the entrance ramp to go east on Interstate 30.

But Hank knew, all too well, that her grief over Ben's death would most likely never dissipate completely. In fact, her loyalty to and depth of emotion for those lucky enough to be let into her inner circle was one of the things he admired the most about her.

Which was why he was determined to make sure that whatever was developing between them moved at a pace Annie felt comfortable with – if, that is, she chose for it to develop further at all. Although she'd mentioned needing to talk about things, she hadn't brought it up, not once, in the roughly four weeks since he'd taken that chance and kissed her.

And he wasn't about to press the matter.

Hank was so deep in thought he almost missed the exit he needed. He noticed just in the nick of time and guided his truck down the off ramp, then left at the stoplight. Hank followed the same route they'd used the prior night to arrive outside her apartment building. He parked his truck, then glanced at his watch.

Seven minutes early. Plenty of time.

He got out and opened the drivers' side back door, then went to work wrestling the presents he'd bought her into the oversized gift bag. Once all four items were neatly tucked away into the festively patterned bag, he lifted it out by the handles and shut the door. Then he reached into the cab via the driver's seat and grabbed the pastry box from the center console.

Hank locked his truck and strolled up the narrow concrete walkway to Annie's front door, shifting the cronut box and gift bag straps into one hand so he could ring the doorbell with the other one.

"Hi, tiny," he said softly and smiled when she opened the door.

Her petite frame was covered in yoga pants and an oversized t-shirt, and he noticed that although she'd wound her still damp hair up into a messy bun of sorts, tiny tendrils were left loose to softly frame her face.

"Morning," she replied, and her grin widened into a beaming smile when she noticed the box.

"You brought cronuts?"

"I had to. It's kind of our thing, you know?" he teased.

Annie giggled. "Yep. Come on in."

She stood aside so he could enter, then closed the door behind him.

"How'd you sleep?" he asked as he strode toward the kitchen.

"Like the dead," she quipped as she followed him, then pounced on the pastry box the moment he set it down. "But getting up this morning really hurt. I spent a good ten minutes extra in the shower just letting the hot water beat down on me so I could limber up enough to move around. And that was *after* wrestling the shower curtain up and onto the rod."

"Well then, I think you'll appreciate my housewarming gifts," he answered as he held up the bag, distracting her from reaching for a cronut.

"Hank. You didn't have to do that."

"I'm aware. But I wanted to do that, so, I did."

"What is it?"

"Just open the thing and find out."

She closed the distance and took the bag from him with her left hand, then reached down into it with her right.

"Epsom salts! Nice," she remarked as she pulled the first piece of the puzzle up into view and set it on the counter.

The exclamation of 'Ooh, lavender!' that came next when Annie brought forth the scented candle and bath bomb made him chuckle.

"The last thing is big. What did you do?" she queried as she set the bag on the floor so she could use both hands to pull up on the box.

"You'll see."

Annie finally worked it free of the bag, and grinned.

"Shiatsu shoulder and back massager – with heat," she read

aloud, and smiled up at him. "Heck yes! That's gonna feel *so* good later."

She carefully set the box down, then stood on tiptoe to kiss his cheek.

"Thank you. I really appreciate the gifts, and I will make good use of them."

"You're welcome. Now, have a cronut, and let's get a battle plan in place. Which part of all that," - he gestured toward her belongings piled in the living room – "did you want to focus on first?"

She pondered his question while she chewed.

"I'm thinking divide and conquer," she announced in between bites. "Which room do you want to take?"

"I can start on the kitchen," he offered.

"Done. I will start in the bathroom and work my way this way," Annie said. "Just do me a favor, okay? Keep in mind that I'm almost a foot shorter than you when you're shoving things into the top cabinets."

Hank roared with laughter.

"I promise I won't put anything anywhere you need a stepstool to reach, tiny. Fair enough?" he replied, his blue eyes twinkling with mirth.

"Fair enough," Annie decided, and snatched up another cronut before she pivoted to the living room to grab the closest box with bathroom items in it.

Nathan Thomas was amused, and not at all surprised.

Charlie had been remarkably quiet and still – particularly for a four-year-old – for the ninety minutes that graduate after graduate walked across the stage to shake hands and receive their diplomas.

But decorum went out the window once Bella's name was finally read out loud to the previously somber audience.

Charlie promptly stood up on his chair, clapped his hands, and shouted *"Yay, Mommy!!"* at the top of his lungs as his mother, scarlet-faced but smiling, moved hastily forward to shake hands and accept the tangible proof of her success.

There was one pin-drop moment of dead quiet before the entire auditorium erupted with laughter.

The university president, who in his opening remarks had asked that all applause be held until the end, shed his serious expression long enough to show amusement at the enthusiastic outburst.

After a few moments, calm was restored. The few remaining graduates continued through the presentation portion of commencement as Charlie retook his seat, well pleased with his supportive efforts.

Within fifteen minutes, it was over, and Bella's family waited as she made her way through the throng to where they were sitting.

"Did you hear me? Did you hear me, Mommy? I clapped for you!" Charlie exclaimed as he launched himself into her arms.

"Yes, you did, and it was awesome. I love you, Charlie," Bella replied, and kissed him on the forehead before she turned her attention to Nathan, Jandy, Rick, and Faith.

"I don't know about you guys, but I feel like celebrating – and I'm starving," she announced with a sparkle in her eye. "How about we start with lunch?"

Nathan wrapped his arm around her waist. "Anywhere you want to go, baby. Anywhere you want to go."

"Mac and cheese?" Charlie asked hopefully, and made his family laugh all over again.

Chapter Two

By LUNCHTIME, Lizzie had to admit that the ginger tea had worked wonders.

She was happily sprawled out on the couch in the living room, watching television with Donny and enjoying the fact that her nausea had been banished, if only temporarily.

So much so, in fact, that she opted to give in to her sudden craving.

"I want a pretzel," she announced suddenly. "One of those big soft ones that they serve with the cheese sauce to dip it in. Matter of fact, I want *three* of them. Where do they sell those?"

Donny blinked several times.

"But I thought you didn't like pretzels."

She shrugged, then grinned and rubbed her stomach.

"Evidently I do now."

"I have no idea where to get some," he said as he stood up. "But I'm about to find out. Let me grab my laptop."

Hank and Annie took a break around two p.m., and she stood with her hands on her hips and surveyed the progress.

"Not too shabby!" she pronounced. "At this rate, I will actually be able to sit and relax at least part of tomorrow."

Hank grinned.

"Well, that's the goal, isn't it. To have at least a little sliver of weekend left to just relax. But food should be a priority, too. Wanna order some sandwiches, or a pizza?"

"Sandwiches work for me."

"Good," he replied, and scrolled through his cell phone, then handed it to her.

"Here's the menu. Pick out what you want, then click 'add'. I've already got my sandwich in the cart."

Annie reviewed his selection.

"The one you chose sounds delicious. Let's just make it two of those," she told him, and increased the quantity before she handed him back his phone.

Hank added chips and drinks to their order, then clicked 'submit'.

"Okay, should be here in about a half-hour," he announced. "What's next?"

"Well, we've gotten the bathroom, kitchen, my room, and my office squared away. The last big pieces left are the things that go in the entertainment center and the bookshelves and making a trip to the grocery store. I can hang pictures and do the decorative bit little by little over the next few weeks."

"I'll take filling the bookshelves if you'll handle unpacking what goes in the entertainment center," Hank suggested. "And we should probably make the store trip *after* we eat lunch. Could get expensive otherwise."

"Don't I know it."

They got to work on the living room, and as they unpacked her things and restored them to their proper places, the burning question that had been circling Annie's mind for the last month surfaced front and center once more.

So... about what happened at the cabin, was what she wanted to say.

"So... how's the new job going?" is what she heard herself ask instead, and thought, *way to chicken out.*

"I love it. Really glad I made the change," Hank replied with a grin as he picked up another armful of books and set them on a shelf.

"That's great!"

"I thought so, too," he agreed. "I know I just started there, but already I feel like I'm doing some good. And it's straightforward, you know? No having to pretend to be something or someone I'm not. It's a refreshing change."

"What do you mean?"

"Well, when I was DEA I had to go undercover on assignments. I hated it, especially the long-term ones. I was good at it - extremely good at it, actually – but I hated it. After a while the line between what's fake and what's real can be blurry."

There was a long pause, and she glanced over to see him frowning at the books in his hand.

"It takes a toll," he finally continued as he placed them on the shelf. "You're always looking over your shoulder. When you're in character you can never really relax, not completely, because losing your focus can get you killed."

"I felt that way both times I went undercover, even though each time it wasn't more than an hour or two," Annie confessed quietly. "I can't even imagine the stress of doing it for an extended period."

She set the small stack of DVD's down, crossed over to stand in front of him, and shocked him by wrapping her arms around his waist.

"I'm glad you made the change, too," she said, then laid her head on his chest and hugged him.

"I never told anyone that before," Hank admitted as he folded his arms around her to return the hug. "I don't know why it is that you're so easy to talk to, Annie, but I'm grateful for it."

He looked down at the same moment she looked up, and their

eyes locked and held. Time seemed to stop cold as Hank began to lean down, and all Annie could think about was that a second kiss between them could happen at any moment.

And she realized she was more than just okay with that.

As she slowly went up onto her tiptoes to close the distance faster, her doorbell rang, startling them both and shattering the moment.

"Oh," Annie blurted out in surprise. "That must be the food. I'll get it."

She blushed as she wriggled out of his embrace to answer the door.

"You can take that off now," Bella told her son when they arrived home, and he squealed and pulled off his clip-on tie.

"Here, buddy, let me help," Nathan said with a chuckle when he saw Charlie struggling with the buttons on his pint-sized dress shirt. "What shirt do you want to change into?"

"Dinosaurs," came the swift reply.

"You got it. Let's go hang this one up first," Nathan told him as they walked side-by-side down the hall and out of sight.

Bella sighed and leaned against the kitchen counter.

I can't believe I'm finally done, she mused as she looked down at the Master of Arts certificate she held in her hands.

She was, she realized suddenly, both excited and terrified at the prospect of running an interview gauntlet in the coming weeks. While she was supremely confident in her abilities, Bella was also grounded enough to realize that her relevant work history to date had been mighty sparse.

The Metzger Institute. That's just about it for hands-on work in my field – and after what came to light, I'm not sure I even want it showing on my resume!

She sighed again.

"What's wrong?" Nathan asked as he came into the kitchen.

"Where's Charlie?"

"Cartoons," Nathan answered, and motioned over his shoulder. "Trust me, he's set. What's going on?"

"Well," she began, "I think it's finally sinking in that I'm done with school. And I have all these interviews lined up, and I'm grateful for that. I'm just concerned that my skills alone won't be enough. The only job I've had that pertained directly to languages was The Metzger Institute, and…".

Her voice trailed off.

"And because of Adolf and Mikel Metzger, you're concerned that listing that place on any resumes you hand out is a detriment, not an asset."

"*Exactly.*"

"I can see your concern," he commiserated. "And to be honest, honey, I'm not sure about it, either. When is your first interview?"

"Tuesday."

"Okay," Nathan said. "I think you should call the university and talk to someone at the Career Development Center. Run it by them and see what advice they have. You might be psyching yourself out for no reason."

He gathered her into a slow kiss.

"In the meantime," he murmured, "I am so damn proud of you, Bella. You're an amazing woman, and Charlie and I are lucky to have you in our lives."

"Sweet talker," Bella whispered. "Keep going, I like it."

"Mom! Dad! Come see!" came the yelled request from the living room.

Bella and Nathan sighed in unison.

"Tell you what. Once we get little man down for the night, let's plan on soak time," he said, and wiggled his eyebrows at her.

"Deal."

An awkward silence reigned as Annie and Hank ate their sandwiches, then resumed restoring order to her living room. By four p.m. the only major task that remained was the grocery store trip.

It wasn't until they'd gone halfway down the fourth aisle that the atmosphere between them snapped back to normalcy.

"You're going to need mayo," he said, and Annie shuddered.

"Ew. Why? That stuff's gross."

"You don't like mayo? I'm sorry, tiny, but that's a dealbreaker. We can no longer be friends," Hank teased, then made a show of walking to the end of the aisle before he stopped, turned around, and smiled at her.

Annie rolled her eyes and fought back the urge to snicker.

"Fine. If it's that big a deal to you, I'll grab a little jar of that stuff. For when I have company."

He strode back her direction with a mischievous smirk.

"Don't buy it on my account," he said casually. "That stuff's nasty. I just wanted to see what you'd do."

Hank spent the length of the next aisle rubbing his arm where she'd playfully smacked him. But his teasing had the effect he'd hoped for; the tension between them had melted away.

"Man," Annie said as they wheeled the full cart toward the checkout lanes. "Been a while since I had to stock up a place from scratch. I'm glad I only have to do this once."

They worked in tandem to unload the cart's items onto the short conveyor belt for the cashier to scan, and the moment the cart was empty Hank pushed it forward and assumed bagging duties at the other end. By the time the last item had cleared the scanning pad, Annie's groceries were mostly contained in bags and already nestled back into the cart.

Annie settled the bill, took the receipt the cashier offered, then looked at Hank.

"Shall we?"

"After you," he answered with a grin.

Outside, they loaded up Hank's back seat from both sides, then stowed the now empty cart in the closest cart corral before they made the drive back to her apartment.

By the time the last canned good was put away it was just after seven o'clock.

"Want to stay for dinner?" she asked. "I can make spaghetti."

"Sure," Hank replied. "But only if you let me help."

"Sounds like a deal to me."

Petite, bubbly Hollie Blumfeld, a twenty-two-year-old political science major at the University of Texas in Arlington, rubbed her eyes and yawned.

"May I have your attention, please. The library will be closing in ten minutes."

Hollie closed her textbook and frowned when she heard the automated announcement.

"Almost eight o'clock already?" she muttered as she glanced at her watch. "Dammit. All right. Guess I'd better get moving."

It's a good thing Clarissa is staying over at Brett's tonight. I can get some decent sleep, at least, she mused to herself as she stood, stretched, then gathered her belongings.

Not that she begrudged her best friend's happiness, at all. She just didn't appreciate being kept awake by their... enthusiasm that tended to last well into the wee hours of the morning.

The apartment's bedrooms aren't exactly soundproofed, she acknowledged with a wry grin as she strode away from the little alcove she'd claimed as her study area four hours earlier.

Hollie waved goodbye to the clerk manning the circulation desk as she walked past it and stepped through the double doors and out into the night air.

Hefting her backpack onto her slender shoulders, she quickly made her way down the wide steps and headed west toward her off-campus apartment, her long blond ponytail swinging back and forth as she moved along the well-tended path.

"Hey, Hollie," she heard someone call out, and she glanced to her left and smiled.

"Hey, Angie," she answered as her classmate fell into step beside her. "Let me guess. You didn't have anything better to do on a Saturday night, either."

"Oh, I did," Angie replied. "I just needed to get my last paper knocked out first. And now that it's done, I'm heading out to celebrate. Wanna come? Some of us are gonna go check out that new dance club."

"I appreciate the invite, but I'm wiped out. Rain check?"

"You sure? If *I* were only one semester away from being done, I'd party up a storm."

Hollie shrugged even as she grinned.

"No rest for the wicked, I guess."

"Well, you change your mind, you know where we'll be," Angie told her as she veered off toward the parking lot on the south side of the path. "See you later."

"Have fun."

Hollie continued westward until she reached the edge of campus, then looked both ways before she crossed the two-lane street toward the old Victorian-style house that had been converted from a single-family home into a three-unit apartment building.

"Hey there Sasha," she crooned to the tabby cat who'd leapt up into the windowsill and mewed loudly as Hollie retrieved her keys. "Hang on, I'm coming."

She unlocked the door, stepped inside, and closed it behind her. But her forward motion into the apartment was disrupted by Sasha, who'd jumped back down onto the floor, scampered over to the door, and began weaving herself between Hollie's feet.

"You're going to trip me, you silly thing," Hollie observed with a laugh as she shuffled her way to the coffee table to set down her backpack.

That accomplished, she scooped up a persistent Sasha, who trilled in anticipation of both affection and food.

"Okay, angel baby," she cooed as she stroked Sasha's head. "How about we get you some kibble?"

The cat responded with an increasingly loud purr and a lazy headbutt to Hollie's chin as they moved together toward the kitchen.

Hollie set Sasha on the floor, retrieved a can of Fancy Feast from the cupboard, and waved it at the cat.

"How about tuna in gravy?" she asked, then laughed when Sasha meowed like she'd not been fed in days.

The noise didn't abate until Hollie set the tiny plate down on the floor where Sasha could reach it.

"You're welcome, Your Highness," Hollie remarked while her pet completely ignored her and concentrated on the food. "You enjoy that. I'm heading for a shower."

She turned and made her way down the hall to her bedroom, where she gathered up her sleep shirt and shorts, then padded into the bathroom.

Hollie started the shower, undressed, then took down her ponytail and brushed out her hair while she waited for the water to come up to temperature. After a couple of minutes, she pulled back the curtain and stepped over the clawfoot tub's side to duck her head under the spray.

She'd just lathered up her hair when she heard a commotion beyond the bathroom door. Sasha was hissing and snarling – sounds Hollie had never heard her make before.

Concerned, she stepped out of the shower, grabbed a towel, and quickly wrapped it around her body.

"Sasha! You all right?" she called out as she flung open the bathroom door.

But she never got a chance to check on the beloved pet she'd had for seven years. The first strike of the killer's blade struck deep and true, piercing Hollie Blumfeld's heart and sealing her fate.

She stumbled back from the blow's force, her arms raised to ward off her assailant. Her towel slipped to the floor unnoticed, and her eyes went wide with abject shock and terror as Hollie glanced down at the knife protruding from her chest, then back up at her killer. She'd just opened her mouth to try to scream when the tub's edge caught her just above the back of her knees and sent her toppling over backward.

Her murderer closed the small gap between them, and the other fifteen knife wounds inflicted after Hollie lay crumpled and defenseless in the tub were merely for show.

Chapter Three

By the time Sunday morning came around, Bella Thomas had decided to also get her best friend Stacy's take on the situation.

"So, what do you think?" Bella asked.

"I think you should list it, Bel," Stacy answered immediately. "For several reasons. Wait, hang on a second."

Bella heard her say, "Emily Grace! *No, ma'am!* Put those back!" and chuckled to herself.

"Sorry about that," Stacy explained. "My child has decided she wants to be a paleontologist. Which is great, except she keeps trying to sneak my ice cream scoop, pastry brush, and pasta strainer into the backyard so she can look for dinosaur bones."

"Huh. Well, then. I guess I know what Auntie Bella can get her for her birthday, then," Bella quipped. "I bet I can find a kid-size set of tools that she'll love."

"And it's a present I will wholeheartedly endorse if it keeps her from rummaging through the kitchen drawers," Stacy said on a sigh. "It's awesome she's so passionate about it, though."

There was a brief pause before Stacy resumed their prior topic of conversation.

"I think you should go ahead and list Metzger Institute on your resume," she announced. "First, you did solid work there. You can expound on Tommy's progress as an example. Second, the folks that stepped in and took those locations over when the crap hit the fan have a long and successful track record of helping at-risk kids. That's gone a long way to repairing the program's reputation."

"Yes, I would think so," Bella agreed.

"Third, it's better to be up front about it, Bel. Any employer worth their salt will run a background check and it will come up anyway. Might as well get it out in the open to begin with. You weren't responsible for what happened there, so you've got nothing to hide."

"Good point," Bella conceded.

"And lastly, it's been how long? Four years, almost five? If a company is going to decide to not hire *you* because of *someone else's* actions five years ago, then that isn't a place you want to work anyway, girl."

"You know what? You're right," Bella decided. "I *did* make some excellent strides with the kids assigned to me. And it's not my fault my employer and his creepy son turned out to be psychopaths. Thanks, Stacy. Talking it out with you was helpful."

"Anytime. Now, on to the next topic – Memorial Day weekend is coming up, and Brad and Emily and I were considering coming into town to hang out with my aunt, but she's already booked a getaway trip with her girlfriends. Some retirement party thing."

"Come to Texas anyway!" was Bella's immediate reply. "You guys can stay with us. We'd love to see you, and I bet Charlie and Emily would have a lot of fun playing together."

Annie Adams arrived at their usual monthly brunch site a little flushed and breathless.

"You all right?" Grace Womack asked her.

"Fine. Overslept," Annie panted as she shrugged off her jacket, took her seat, and reached for the mimosa that the waiter had just placed on the table.

Grace's eyebrow shot skyward as she observed Annie's color continue to deepen.

"Overslept, huh? And did someone keep you up too late?" she teased.

"Uh... well... no," Annie stammered. "Not like you're thinking, anyway."

She frowned, her fingers nervously twisting the cloth napkin at her place setting.

"Then what's going on with you?"

Annie sighed, then tucked her chin.

"I'm not sure what to do," she confided.

"About what?"

"Hank."

"I see," Grace replied smoothly as she looked over the menu. "What about him?"

The conversation lulled when the waiter returned to collect their orders. Once he'd left again, Annie shrugged.

"Okay, so, you know I told you about what happened in Oklahoma," she began.

"I recall."

"And ever since it happened, we have not talked about it. At all."

"And?"

"And, don't you think I should bring it up? I think I should bring it up. But every time I think 'okay, today's the day, I'm gonna ask him what he was thinking' I open my mouth and a totally different subject comes out," Annie confessed, and sagged her shoulders.

"It's this really big elephant in the room every time I am near him, and I feel like we should talk about it."

"I get why you'd feel that way. What I *don't* get," Grace emphasized as she picked up her own mimosa, "is why you're so scared to talk about it. What is the worst that could happen?"

"Well, let's see. He could tell me it was a great big fat mistake, done completely on the spur of the moment," Annie suggested, causing Grace to chuckle.

"Girl. You honestly think that? You're crazy. A man who thought it was a mistake wouldn't look at you like he's dying of thirst and you're a tall, cool glass of water."

Annie scoffed.

"Hank doesn't look at me like that."

"If you honestly think *that*, you haven't been paying attention."

Grace chuckled again when she glanced over and saw Annie's expression.

"I can't tell if you are more hopeful, or terrified."

"Both. I feel both. But – what if you're wrong, Grace? What if he doesn't feel that way about me and that's why he hasn't mentioned anything? Bringing it up could really screw up our friendship."

"You need to ask yourself what is worse – never talking it out and therefore never knowing, or, taking that chance and seeing what happens?"

When Annie started to protest, Grace raised a hand.

"And if you think that your friendship with that man is so weak it can't handle a conversation? Then that's a whole other topic that only you can address."

Hank Myers met his boss in the lobby of Cosantóirí LLC promptly at ten-thirty.

"Sorry to have to tag you on your day off," Allen began as they started the walk side-by-side toward the conference room. "But we've just received a request to provide full security for a client that is coming into town tomorrow, and we need to line out a plan ahead of time."

"Who's the client?"

"Gabe Crosson."

"Gabe Crosson? The best-selling author?"

"The one and only."

"Shouldn't he already have security in place?"

Allen stopped and turned to face him.

"Gabe does – but also thinks one of them might be involved," Allen said, his expression grim. "We're bringing the entire team in on this one. Most of us will be responsible for the physical safety aspects, while one of us ferrets out who the stalker is."

Allen clapped a hand on Hank's shoulder.

"I want you doing the digging. You've been undercover several times in your career, so you know the drill. You're the one I want to plant as a mole in Gabe's entourage, and your single goal is to identify the threat."

With that, he turned and strode into the conference room, leaving Hank in the hallway to absorb what he'd just been told.

***

"Are the potato packets ready?" Lizzie asked her husband a little after noon.

"Just finished them," Donny announced as he folded the foil around the sixth one, then headed to the front door to answer it.

"Hey guys, come on in," he gestured to Faith and Rick.

"We brought a salad and dessert," Faith told him as she kissed his cheek then stepped around him to head to the kitchen.

"And wine," Rick added with a grin, holding the bottle aloft as he followed her.

Faith placed her items on the table so she could hug Lizzie.

"How are you feeling?"

"Still can't have coffee," Lizzie pouted. "But Donny's mom suggested ginger for the nausea, and so far it's working pretty well."

"Well, that's good, right?"

"So far it's been a game-changer. Let's hope the magic doesn't wear off," Lizzie responded with a sigh.

The doorbell chimed again.

"Must be Joe and Trish. I'll get it," Lizzie said to Donny, who had just picked up the tray of potato packets and was beginning to head toward the back door and the grill with Rick.

When she opened the front door, her jaw dropped wide open in surprise.

"*Jones?*"

Her former fellow FBI agent grinned ear to ear.

"Hey, Zim. How you been?"

"Oh, my God. Get in here!" she exclaimed and hugged him. "Donny! Look who's here!"

Lizzie calling him caused Donny to veer her direction.

"Hey, buddy! Long time no see. How are you?"

"I've been good," Jones replied as he hugged Lizzie back, then stepped across the threshold. "Lots to tell you guys. I didn't come at a bad time, did I?"

"Not at all. You want to eat with us? We're just about to fire up the grill," Donny offered.

"Um, sure, if that's all right," Jones replied. "I mean, pretty sure I'm not being tracked this time, so...".

Commotion on the porch caused them all to turn.

"Hi there!" Trish trilled gaily as she and Joe stepped forward and entered the house. "We brought a side dish and some rolls."

"Perfect! Come on in," Lizzie answered, and maneuvered around the small throng to close the door.

"The place looks great," Jones observed as he looked around at the completely renovated home.

"Wait until you see what we did with the kitchen," Lizzie replied with a smile. "Since we had the opportunity anyway, we gave it a major upgrade."

An hour later, as the group at Lizzie's house took their seats around the dining room table, Nathan and Bella's front doorbell pealed twice.

When he opened the door, Nathan was shocked to find a red-eyed and distraught Sarah Thomas standing there with three suitcases.

"Sarah! What's wrong?"

"I got fired. Can I come in?" she asked just before she started to cry.

"Okay, come on, sis," he said gently as he wrapped his arms around her. "It's all gonna be okay, all right?"

He led her to the couch, then returned and retrieved her luggage from the porch. He'd just moved back to sit beside her on the couch when Bella entered the room.

"Oh, honey. What's wrong?" Bella asked her as she swiftly closed the distance to sit on Sarah's other side and clasp her hand.

"The new guy's a douche, that's what's wrong," Sarah managed through her tears. "They hired some punk ass to run the department, and he completely screwed up the summer and fall campaigns, then blamed it all on me. It was my word against his, and I couldn't prove that he was the one responsible."

She took a deep, shuddering breath.

"I busted my ass for those people," Sarah lamented. "I worked my fingers to the freaking *bone* for them. I worked nonstop. I had zero social life. I even missed holidays and family events, and for what? So some jerk who's sleeping with the Vice President can throw me under the bus?"

She hung her head.

"I just... I can't... I don't know what I'm going to do next," she cried. "I got *fired*, and word in this industry spreads really quickly. My entire career is in jeopardy because two idiots are bumping uglies and covering each other's asses."

"Here's what we're going to do," Bella said as she squeezed her sister-in-law's hand. "You're going to stay here for as long as you need to. You're going to take a breath and calm down and realize that yes, you've suffered a setback. But it's not the end, Sarah. Give yourself some time to think things over, and then build a plan to move forward. Right this second, though, you really look like you could use some wine."

"Okay," Sarah answered as she wiped her cheeks. "Okay. All that sounds good. *Especially* the wine."

"I'll take your suitcases to the guest room," Nathan offered. "And then, we'll sit down and talk."

After the others had departed, Lizzie and Donny turned to look at Jones.

"Okay, spill," Lizzie instructed as the three of them settled into the living room. "Not that I'm not happy to see you, but why are you here? And how did you even know it was safe to come back?"

"I talked to my old section chief a couple of weeks ago," Jones revealed. "There's only so much being in tune with nature I can stand. I decided to take a chance and call him to check in on things, and he let me know what went down with the Cortinas cartel. I figure they have other, bigger issues than coming after me, so, I decided to rejoin the world."

He took a sip of his drink.

"And I like this area, so, I started looking through job listings. I have a couple of interviews lined up in the next few days. Cybersecurity. Nothing on the front lines, for which I am extremely grateful. With a little luck, I can shift my career to something that *won't* involve gunfire – or getting anyone's house blown up again."

Donny smirked.

"I think the chances of that happening again are very low, so, you're welcome to stay here with us if you want," he offered after he looked at Lizzie and received her nod of confirmation.

"Thanks, guys. I really appreciate it. And I'll try not to wear out my welcome."

Jones stood and pointed down the hall.

"Guestroom still the second door to the left?"

"Yep. Help yourself."

"Cool. I'm gonna go get my bag. Be right back."

Clarissa Mackabee rested her left hand atop the steering wheel and sang along with the radio as she made her way back to the apartment on Sunday night. Each car's headlights that drove past made her brand-new engagement ring sparkle, and her smile widened more each time.

What a great weekend. I cannot wait to see the look on Hollie's face when I tell her Brett proposed!

She drove along, her head full of dreams of white lace and flowers, already plotting and planning her big day. In no time at all she was pulling into the driveway and turning off the ignition.

Clarissa hummed to herself as she gathered her overnight bag from the front passenger seat, then raced up the front steps and into their first-floor apartment.

"Hollie, I've got the most amazing news!" she called out as she headed down the darkened hall.

She paused outside the bathroom door when she heard the water running.

"Finish your shower, quick! I need to tell you something," Clarissa announced, then listened and waited.

Hearing no reply, she shrugged and continued to her room to drop her bag on her bed, then made her way back to the bathroom door.

"Hollie, I'm serious! I need to talk to you," she said with a laugh as she knocked on the door, then tried the handle.

To her surprise, the door wasn't locked.

That's odd, Clarissa thought. *She always locks the door.*

She grasped the handle and pushed, the door swinging freely open, and entered the small bathroom.

"Okay, so, you're not gonna believe what Brett did this weekend," Clarissa began as she leaned against the bathroom sink. "He asked me! He *finally* asked me! Isn't that great?"

No response.

"Hollie, did you hear what I said? We're engaged!"

No response.

"Damn, girl. At least let me show you this ring."

Met with silence yet again, Clarissa frowned.

"Are you even *listening* to me?" she pouted as she took four steps across the space and yanked open the shower curtain.

But when Clarissa looked down and her eyes locked with Hollie's vacant, filmy ones, she screamed, loud and long. And it didn't register at all with Clarissa when her upstairs neighbors suddenly appeared at her side and eased her back out into the hallway, one of them coaxing her toward the living room while the other dialed nine-one-one.

Chapter Four

Nathan Thomas strolled into the break room with his empty coffee mug on Monday morning and found Lizzie scowling as she filled her own mug with hot water.

"Still can't have coffee, huh?"

"Nope," she growled. "And I cannot *wait* until this part is over."

"Hopefully not much longer," Nathan commiserated, then paused.

"What?"

"What what?" he replied.

"Are you stalling on getting your coffee?"

"Well, yeah," he admitted. "I figured it was kind of mean to pour myself a big old mug of it right in front of you when you can't have any."

"You're right, it is. *Very* mean. But don't let that stop you. We're supposed to meet with the Director in four minutes," Lizzie reminded him.

"All right, fine. But let the record show I was trying to be polite," he rejoined as he picked up the coffeepot and poured.

"Noted and appreciated. So, guess who showed up out of the

blue yesterday?" Lizzie mentioned as she dunked her tea bag into her water.

Nathan glanced in her direction as he reached for the creamer. "No idea."

"Jones," Lizzie announced.

"Really? What brought him out of hiding?"

"He got wind of the cartel's implosion. He's got some interviews lined up around here, so, he's staying with us until he lands a job and can get his own place."

"See you and raise you. My sister Sarah showed up unexpectedly yesterday, too."

"The one who lives in California?"

"Yep."

"And?"

"She got fired."

"Oh, no. What happened?"

Nathan glanced at his watch.

"Remind me to tell you later. We need to get moving if we're gonna be on time."

They hurried down the hallway to the conference room and took their seats beside Annie and Rick just as the Director walked in.

"Morning, all," the Director intoned. "There's quite a bit to cover so let's get started, shall we?"

Over in Pantego, Hank Myers knocked twice, then entered his boss's office.

"Good morning, Hank. I'd like to introduce you to Gabe Crosson," Allen told him as he came around his desk to stand beside the middle-aged woman that had just risen from his visitor's chair. "Ms. Crosson, this is Hank Myers."

She stood, ramrod straight at five-foot-three, her brown eyes shining with a welcoming warmth, her silver-streaked shoulder-length brown hair curling to frame plump cheeks and a dazzling smile.

"Nice to meet you," she said, and extended a slender hand toward a very surprised Hank.

"Likewise," Hank finally managed as he shook it, then moved to take the chair beside hers.

She watched as Hank's eyebrows furrowed in confusion and laughed.

"It's short for Gabriella," she explained. "Back when I waded into the mystery and thriller genre, it was an uphill battle. Women simply couldn't write successful crime thriller stories - supposedly. It was unheard of, according to the old guard."

She leaned forward, her eyes sparkling with mischief.

"So, I went with Gabe instead, determined to show them differently. And it worked. They never knew what hit them."

Hank grinned.

"I like your style."

"Good! Me too," she proclaimed, and leaned back in her chair to address both men at once. "Now, where do we begin?"

Once Allen had settled back in behind his desk he steepled his fingers.

"Ms. Crosson, I've already read Hank into your situation," he began. "The others on my staff will operate in plain sight, acting as your security detail while you're in town. Hank here will be in the background. No one on your current team will know who he is or why he's there."

She smiled and nodded at his words, then cast a sidelong glance at Hank.

"Good to know. I do love a good mystery – made my living writing them. But in real life, it's much scarier than it is exhilarating," she confessed with a wan smile. "Especially when I'm the one being targeted."

"Ms. Crosson," Hank started to say, but she reached over and patted his arm.

"My life is quite literally in your hands. That warrants dropping the formalities, don't you think? Please, call me Gabe."

A yawning Jones shuffled into the living room at Lizzie and Donny's house and waved good morning to Donny before continuing toward the kitchen to get some coffee.

"How'd you sleep?" Donny called out.

"Really well," Jones revealed. "Better than I have in months if I'm being honest. Not having to look over my shoulder anymore makes it easier, I know that much."

Donny chuckled. "I bet."

Jones disappeared and returned a few minutes later with a steaming mug in hand.

"So, what's on tap for you today?"

"Two onboarding meetings with brand new clients," Donny replied. "One in Waxahachie and one in Denton. I'm just waiting for rush-hour traffic to die down before I head out. You?"

"My first interview is today at two o'clock and it's only about fifteen minutes from here," Jones confirmed. "The other two are tomorrow, but they're both over in Dallas. They're all good jobs, but of the three, I'm most excited about the one I'm interviewing for today."

He sat on the couch and grinned at his host.

"I've never been crazy about Dallas traffic," he confided, and made Donny laugh.

"Me either. But it's a necessary evil."

"True enough."

Meanwhile, at Nathan's house, Sarah and Bella were deep in conversation.

"It's weird," Bella admitted. "For the first time in years, I'm not hustling Charlie to day care so I can make it to class on time. That chapter in my life is closed. Finally."

"Bet that feels good."

"It really does," Bella agreed. "But I'm going to cherish this time while it lasts because there's another milestone coming. Charlie will be five next March, which means..."

Her voice trailed off as she got teary.

"Which means he can start school?" Sarah asked with a gasp. "That can't be right! It feels like you just had him a couple of months ago."

"You're telling me," Bella rejoined. "I can't believe my baby boy will be old enough to attend kindergarten. I'm not sure how to feel about it."

"Well, my mind's made up, then," Sarah proclaimed. "I am going to get as much play time with my nephew as possible while I am here."

"He'd love that! How are you with Legos? That's his latest thing." Sarah smiled.

"I can definitely do that."

Charlie appeared at her side, drawn to their conversation by over-hearing the word 'Lego'.

"Come play?" he piped up with a hopeful expression.

"You bet, buddy. Lead the way."

"Yay!" he squealed and ran down the hall to bring forth his bucket of blocks.

***

Over in Mansfield, twenty-five-year-old Sugar Phillips hummed to herself as she dressed for work.

She'd always loved kids, so her chosen career path as a dental hygienist for a well-respected pediatric clinic made her look forward to going to work each morning.

She eased her pink, teddy-bear patterned scrub top down over the insulin pump clipped to her waistband, then checked herself in her bathroom mirror.

"Small price to pay to keep things level," she reminded her reflection.

Sugar had been aptly named. As far back as she could recall, she'd possessed an almost insatiable sweet tooth. As a result, being officially diagnosed with Type-1 diabetes triggered by a severe bout of the flu had been a devastating blow.

The subsequent years had been rough to say the least. Her struggle to be consistent with her medication and stay away from the sugary concoctions she loved had eventually resulted in being fitted with an insulin pump just before the new year.

She didn't care for it one bit, but if it kept her alive and healthy...

It is what it is, Sugar told herself as she reached for her toothbrush to complete her morning routine.

A few minutes later, she hustled to the kitchen to pack herself a sack lunch, then grabbed her purse and keys and left the house.

Sugar's commute was also something she loved about her job – a mere eight miles from her driveway to the office's parking lot – and she congratulated herself heartily when she conquered the temptation to stop at the donut shop on her way to work.

She pulled into her designated spot at ten minutes to eight, whistling to herself as she gathered up her belongings and walked into the building to start her day.

"Good morning, ya'll," Sugar called out to her co-workers as she made her way to the small employee lounge to put her lunch in the refrigerator and her other belongings in her locker.

That done, she walked to the front desk area to review which patients were scheduled to come in first. A few minutes later, she stepped through the door separating the waiting room from the treatment rooms, unlocked the door, and flipped the sign from 'closed' to 'open'.

The first patient to arrive was Jonas, a vibrant six-year-old that was one of Sugar's personal favorites.

"Good morning," she beamed at him and his mother. "Nice to see you guys! You ready, Jonas?'

He reached up and clasped her hand.

"Yes, Miss Sugar."

When their planning meeting was done, Hank Myers stepped out into the hall to reach out to Annie. They'd made plans to have dinner, but Hank's new assignment meant things would have to be postponed.

He dialed her number and waited as the line rang four times, then went to voicemail.

"Hi," he said once the beep had sounded. "I hate to do this, but I've got an assignment, and I have no idea what the week's gonna look like. Can we rain check dinner tonight? I'm so sorry, Annie. I'll make it up to you, I promise. I've got to go but I'll try my best to call this week, all right? Catch you later."

He hung up, shoved his cell phone back in his pocket, and turned around to find Gabe watching him with a mischievous grin.

"If you love her, you should tell her," Gabe told him, and caught him completely off guard.

He felt his cheeks turn a little red as he stammered a response.

"I don't... I mean... We just...".

She clucked her tongue and shook her head at him.

"I didn't always write thrillers, you know. I got my start in romance. I can tell when a guy's hung up on a woman – and I can tell that you are head over heels for that one. Life's too short, Hank. Tell her how you *feel*."

She patted his arm and nodded, then walked past him and through the door that Allen was holding open for her.

Hank watched the door close behind them and sighed as he mulled over Gabe Crosson's advice.

Tell Annie how I feel. So simple - yet so difficult.

"Rick sure looked happy," Lizzie mentioned as she picked at the chef salad she'd ordered for lunch.

"Definitely. He lives and breathes that stuff," Nathan affirmed.

During the morning meeting, the Director had assigned Rick Conner as lead agent on a new case that heavily involved encryption – namely, tracing, intercepting, and decoding viable evidence with which to obtain arrest warrants. Rick had grinned like a kid at Christmas when he'd been given the task of playing cyber detective once again.

"Did he ever tell you *why* he changed his mind about joining us full-time, exactly?"

"Nope," Nathan said with a shrug. "But I asked him to every chance I got, so, I am assuming that I just wore him down finally."

He noticed Lizzie's frown.

"What's wrong?"

"This salad is missing something, but I can't figure out what."

"Huh?"

"It just doesn't taste right."

"O...kay.. this isn't one of those weird craving things, is it? Because I'm honestly surprised that you ordered a salad to begin with when you usually get the chicken fried steak."

"I know. Me too," Lizzie confirmed, still scowling as she moved the ingredients around. "And it's what I wanted, but something's missing."

After several moments, Lizzie's face lit up with happiness.

"I know what it needs!" she exclaimed.

Nathan held his hands up in an 'I surrender' pose.

"I don't really think I want to know, Liz."

He cringed, then heaved a sigh of relief when she called the waitress over and asked for tabasco sauce.

"Okay, that's actually not too weird – other than the fact that you don't like spicy food, usually."

"Nope, not usually," she agreed with a grin. "Then again, Donny tracked down soft pretzels for me this weekend because I *had* to have them – and I hate pretzels. Go figure."

Once she'd spruced up her salad with the tabasco sauce she'd requested, Lizzie gestured to Nathan.

"So, tell me. What happened with Sarah?"

At the Tarrant County Medical Examiner's office, Dr. Jerry Broder powered through a sandwich and coffee before he left the relative calm of his desk.

Once he'd returned to the autopsy room, he slipped a fresh surgical gown over his scrubs, pulled on fresh gloves, and crossed the space to table three where his next case awaited him.

He yawned again as he walked, causing a heartfelt "Man, I feel that," from his assistant Isaac, who yawned in response.

A violent stomach flu had rampaged through the building; Broder and Isaac were among the small handful of staff members that hadn't succumbed to the illness in the past four days. The result was double shifts for those still healthy enough to work to try to keep up with the steady inflow of cases, and all were beginning to feel the strain.

"Surely there will be a reprieve at some point," Broder muttered as he added a face shield to his ensemble, then switched on the tiny light at the front of his headlamp.

"Let's begin," he announced, nodding at Isaac to start the recorder that would capture all verbal observations for later transcription.

"Hollie Blumfeld, aged twenty-two, Caucasian female. Blond hair, blue eyes, five feet two inches tall and...".

Broder trailed off as he glanced over at a screen hooked to the electronic scale built into the table.

"One hundred one pounds," he continued. "Obvious physical trauma to the chest, abdomen, and thighs."

He sighed.

"Overkill, especially for such a tiny little thing. I count no fewer than sixteen separate penetrating wounds consistent with a thin, tapering blade, but... no noticeable defensive wounds at all," he noted as he closely examined her hands and fingernails.

He obtained her liver temperature, frowned, and glanced up at Isaac.

"Where was she found, exactly?"

Isaac grabbed the file containing scene notes.

"In the bottom of her bathtub, according to this. The shower was running, but her body only partially obstructed the drain, so she wasn't fully submerged."

"Ah, that makes sense. Factoring that in, her liver temperature and overall rigor are consistent with an approximate time of death between eight pm and midnight Saturday."

Isaac jotted that information down, then set the file aside again.

"Let's get pictures and collect any trace evidence and a blood sample, and then we'll clean her up a bit so we can properly measure and catalogue these wounds," Broder directed.

"Yes, sir."

Chapter Five

ANNIE HAD BEEN so focused on her current case assignment that she'd missed Hank's call. It was almost four o'clock before she even realized she had a new voicemail.

As she listened to it, then texted a short reply, she glanced up to see Grace approaching her desk.

"What's with the face?" Grace asked her as Annie set the phone down.

"Dinner's been postponed indefinitely," Annie revealed. "Evidently, he's got something major going on at work."

"Girl. Is that all? You looked like you just found out there's no Santa Claus," Grace rejoined, and shook her head.

"The two of you need to talk about this. *Soon.*"

"I know," Annie confessed, ducking her chin under Grace's intense, no-nonsense gaze. "That's why I had planned to bring it up tonight."

She shrugged her shoulders.

"Guess it will just have to wait a little longer."

Four hours after her autopsy began, Hollie Blumfeld's body was wrapped and scheduled for transport to the funeral home of her family's choice.

While Isaac readied the next case, Broder took a few minutes to enjoy yet another cup of coffee – and to call his wife Ginny to tell her that with any luck, he *might* be home in time for dinner.

Coffee cup empty, he stood, stretched, and left his office to head toward what he sincerely hoped would be the last autopsy to round out a thirteen-hour workday.

"And who do we have here?" he asked once he'd properly suited up again.

"How did your interview go?" Donny asked after he finally returned home from the meeting up in Denton that had run forty minutes longer than he planned.

"I was there for an hour and a half," Jones responded. "I'm guessing that's a good thing? But who knows. I mean, I *feel* like it went well, but I guess I'll find out soon enough. In the meantime, I'd like to make dinner for you guys, if that's all right. As a thanks for letting me stay."

"Knock yourself out, man."

"I'm glad you said that – because I stopped by the store on the way home. Got everything I needed to make chicken marsala."

"Liz will love that! She's a big fan of Italian food. She should be home just anytime now - unless she caught a case," Donny advised as he checked his phone for messages.

"But, no messages, so I'm guessing she didn't. She usually texts to let me know when she'll be late."

He started to dial her number just as she walked through the front door.

"Hey, hon. Jones offered to cook," he exclaimed. "He's making chicken marsala."

"Yum! Works for me. I'm headed to the shower," Lizzie replied as she made her way across the living room.

"Want some company?" Donny murmured as he followed.

"You know it," came the throaty reply, and she took his hand and led him down the hallway.

"Dinner will be ready in about forty minutes," Jones called after them.

"That should be enough time, right?" Lizzie whispered as she looked back and wiggled her eyebrows at her husband.

"I bet we can make that work, yeah," he said casually, and made her laugh out loud.

Bella was surprised to see Nathan arrive home before six p.m.

"Quiet day?"

"Better than average," he replied with a grin as he set down his briefcase. "Mostly wrapping up documentation to turn over to the D.A.'s office. How were things here?"

"Good," she proclaimed. "Charlie and Sarah got some playtime in and had a blast. Meanwhile, I've been trying to prepare for that interview tomorrow, but I am super nervous, Nathan. After dinner, do you think we could do a mock interview? I could use the practice."

He moved to her side to wrap his arm around her.

"Absolutely."

It was a little past seven by the time Broder and his assistant completed the last autopsy of the day, and the exhausted coroner had every intention of retreating to his office to dictate his formal observations on the Blumfeld case.

But he yawned yet again as he walked, and that changed his mind.

I'll do better in the morning with a clear head, he told himself, so instead of settling in at his computer, he logged off and shut it down, grabbed his briefcase, and called Ginny to let her know he was on his way home.

He got only halfway there before he got a call requesting his presence at a new crime scene.

With a heavy sigh, Broder diverted toward his new destination in Mansfield, using his hands-free setup to warn Ginny he'd been wrong yet again about his arrival time as he drove.

Hank Myers settled in at his kitchen table with a takeout burger and his laptop and began to plot out his approach.

Gabe Crosson had turned over every threatening letter and email she'd received to date. While the entire team had been briefed on the situation – namely, that based on those threats, a physical attack on the author could happen at the five-day-long book fair she was in town for – Hank had been charged with becoming a ghost to ferret out *precisely* who wished the woman harm.

His boss had already discreetly contacted the book fair's organizer, who'd agreed to place Hank on the event's official staffing roster. This would provide him with a valid reason to mix and mingle throughout the book fair's run. Now Hank just needed to build a workable plan to blend in - and dig for information.

This thing kicks off Wednesday morning, he confirmed as he skimmed the fair's published schedule of events, making note of the individual sessions that Gabe Crosson was featured as a speaker.

Let's see. Two presentations geared toward authors only, and a third scheduled for Sunday afternoon that would be open to authors and readers alike...

He paused and considered it.

If it were me, I'd want her death to be as public as possible, he mused after he'd closed his eyes and slipped into the stalker's mind-set. *I'd wait until Sunday, when she's thinking the danger is past, then strike while she's up on the stage.*

Of course, based on the hate mail she's gotten, it seems that whoever's after her doesn't even realize Gabe isn't a man...

Hank frowned.

Which means if someone in her circle is involved in this at all, it's by proxy, at best...

Armed with this realization, he hunched over his keyboard and began to plan for two very different scenarios – the less likely but still possible betrayal from within Gabe's ranks, and a mysterious outsider.

Meanwhile, Annie half-heartedly flipped channels until she stumbled across a rerun of *Friends*, then twirled her fork into the leftover spaghetti that she'd heated up for dinner.

Doing that immediately sent her thoughts back to Saturday night, when she and Hank had stood side-by-side to make the meal. Hank had surprised her with remarkably quick and precise chopping skills, easily dicing the onion she'd handed him into perfectly even pieces in no time.

She'd raised an eyebrow, and he'd shrugged, then grinned.

"Once upon a time, I wanted to be a chef," he confessed. "And I watch a lot of cooking shows. I just don't cook, usually. Too much effort for just one person."

"Huh. Good to know. What other surprises do you have up your sleeve?" she'd teased.

"You'll find out soon enough," he'd replied, a mysterious twinkle coming into his blue eyes before he'd changed the subject entirely.

That would have been another great time to get this conversation over with, had I not been such a big chicken, she scolded herself. *And now he's on assignment and there's no telling when I'll even see him again, much less have enough time to talk things out.*

She set her jaw with determination.

We will have to make *time, that's all. Just a question of when.*

Slightly mollified, Annie's attention returned to the TV screen.

A tired Jerry Broder stood and removed his gloves as he pronounced the man sprawled at his feet officially dead, then gestured across the body to the detective that had summoned him to the scene.

"I won't know anything more than what I've just told you until I do the autopsy and run some labs," he said. "And I'll start that in the morning. Not much more I can do tonight."

He turned to look at the two overnight-shift morgue transport techs that had also managed to dodge the stomach ailment cutting a swath through his employees.

"He's all yours. Goodnight, gentlemen."

And with that, Broder trudged back to his SUV for the drive home and a long-awaited dinner, shower, and bed.

"I think you're going to do brilliantly tomorrow," Nathan reassured his wife as they left his home office to rejoin Charlie and Sarah in the living room.

"You think so?"

"I really do. You maintained eye contact and answered each question well – not too much detail, not too little, and you stayed on topic. I think the only thing holding you back is your self-confidence, honey. You've got this. Just be yourself."

Bella smiled.

"Thanks, babe."

"Anytime. Hey Charlie! Ready for bath time?" he called out just as his office phone rang.

"Go. I've got bath time covered," Bella urged, and Nathan pivoted to return to his office to take the call.

———

"Licorice," Lizzie said abruptly as she and Donny worked as a unit to clean the kitchen after dinner since Jones had put together the meal.

"What?"

"Licorice," she repeated, and grinned at the confused look on Donny's face as it morphed into understanding.

"Red or black?"

"Black. And yes, I hate that stuff, and yes, I know it's weird. But I've *got* to have some."

He leaned over and kissed her forehead.

"Then I will be right back. Anything else you want?"

"We have any peanut butter?"

"Yep, a whole unopened jar of it."

"Then nope, just the licorice, please."

"You're right, this is weird."

"You're telling me. This kid won't let me have any coffee *and* it's making me eat salads and pretzels and black licorice? Rude. Just rude."

Their back and forth was interrupted by her cell phone ringing.

"Hey Nathan! What's up?" she said, then listened for a few minutes.

"Sure! I'll be right over," she finished, and hung up.

"I need to head to Nathan's. Steve's supposed to be calling in about a half-hour, and Nathan wants me there," she explained.

"Understood. So, I will meet you back here, I guess."

"*We'll* meet you back here," Jones chimed in from the doorway. "Donny, if you don't mind I'd like to tag along. I have a great idea for dinner tomorrow night, so I was about to make a trip to the store anyway."

"Works for me," Donny answered.

Sugar stood at her kitchen sink, washing dishes and grumbling to herself after a dinner of broiled salmon and steamed vegetables.

"I know eating like this is better for me but man, I'd *kill* for a banana split right about now," she muttered under her breath as she scrubbed, rinsed, and dried her plate and cookware.

She dried off her hands, draped the dishtowel back over the oven door handle, then pivoted over to the fridge.

"Sugar free chocolate pudding," she murmured as she gazed at the top shelf's items. "Guess that will have to do."

She grabbed one, closed the refrigerator door, and retrieved a spoon from the drawer before heading into the living room to relax for a while.

Sugar idly flipped channels as she savored each spoonful of her dessert. When it was gone, she sighed.

"Shower time, I guess," she remarked as she threw away the empty pudding container, then washed and rinsed her spoon.

When she reached her bedroom, Sugar disconnected her insulin pump and set it on top of her dresser, then grabbed clean underwear and a sleep shirt and made her way to the bathroom.

Twenty minutes later she toweled off, put on her nightclothes, and blow dried her hair, then returned to her bedroom. Sugar reattached her insulin pump and clipped it to her long shirt before she turned off the light and climbed into bed.

She never noticed that her insulin pump wasn't *quite* in the same place she'd left it when she'd gone to take her shower.

And a few hours later, once her pump had delivered the massive doses for which it had been reprogrammed, Sugar had no one to call out to for help, even if she'd been able.

Chapter Six

"Don't be nervous. You're going to be great today," Nathan remarked as he watched Bella brush out her long black hair, then turn and go into her closet to decide what to wear for her interview.

"Right this minute, it's equal parts nervous and excited," she answered as she moved hangers of clothes back and forth, then finally settled on a black pantsuit and royal blue blouse.

"This is the job I'm most interested in," Bella confided when she returned to the bathroom and began to dress, starting with the pants. "Being a translator for a major player in the publishing industry would be really cool."

"It does sound cool. And I have every confidence you'd be a rock star at it."

She blushed as she buttoned up her blouse.

"Well, you're a little biased, Mr. Thomas."

"Oh, I definitely am, *Mrs.* Thomas," he answered, then held her suit jacket up for her so she could slide it on. "But that doesn't mean I'm wrong."

"Thanks. How do I look?" she asked and made a slow turn in front of him.

"You look amazing. Very professional."

"Good!"

She glanced at her watch, then moved back into her closet to pick out which shoes to pair with the outfit.

"My interview's not until ten, so I can afford to wait for rush-hour traffic to lighten up a little before I leave, don't you think?" she called out.

Nathan tilted his head.

"It's in downtown Dallas, right?"

"Yep."

"I think if you leave here by eight-forty-five or so, you'll be in good shape."

"Fair enough," she said as she stepped out of her closet, sat on the bed, and slipped on her low-heeled pumps.

Then Bella made her way across the room to kiss him.

"Speaking of time, shouldn't *you* get going?"

"I was just about to grab Charlie and take him to daycare, yes," he replied. "But I wanted to spend a few minutes alone with my wife first."

One searing kiss later, he reluctantly turned Bella loose and stepped back.

"Okay, I really should get going," he said with a grin. "See you tonight."

She watched him walk out of the room, then whirled around and marched back into her closet, second-guessing the pantsuit she'd picked out.

By eight-fifteen Bella had cycled through four more possible outfits before she discarded them all in favor of the initial one she'd chosen.

Well, that was an exercise in futility, she acknowledged as she sat down on the corner of the bed and put the first pair of low-heeled shoes on again. *But it's better to work out some of the nerves here rather than carry them into my interview, I suppose.*

Strangely comforted by that thought, Bella made her way to her kitchen for a cup of hot tea.

A sleepy Sarah greeted her as she entered the kitchen.

"You look great! How are you feeling?"

"Nervous," Bella admitted as she poured hot water into her mug.

After a few minutes spent enjoying her tea and chatting with her sister-in-law, it was time to get going.

"Wish me luck!" Bella said as she grabbed her purse, keys, and the slender binder that contained resumé copies and a pad and pen.

"Just be you. You've got this."

Bella smiled.

"I appreciate the support."

Within twenty minutes she was glad she'd taken her husband's advice about the timing of her departure. While traffic hadn't completely dissipated, it was lighter than she'd expected; the thirty-mile drive into the heart of downtown Dallas only took fifty minutes.

"Now, to find parking," she muttered to herself as she scanned the lots around the building she needed to go to.

Ten minutes elapsed before she found a space five blocks away.

"Glad I went with low heels!" she remarked as she pulled into the space and killed the engine.

Bella took a moment to text Nathan and let him know she'd arrived safely before she scooped up her purse and binder and stepped out of her SUV.

She'd no sooner locked her vehicle when her phone chimed with his response.

Good luck, honey! Love you!

Love you too, she typed back, then put her phone in her purse and began to walk southwest toward her destination – and noticed that the stark grey multi-story building that housed the FBI's field office was only two blocks up on the right.

At ten minutes to ten Bella was signed in with the company's receptionist and took a seat in the lobby to wait. She retrieved her phone and fired off another quick text to Nathan.

This place is only three blocks from your building. Want to have lunch together today?

As before, his response was immediate.

Absolutely. Call me when you're done.

She made sure that her phone's ringer was muted and tucked it back into her purse just before a woman approached her position.

"Bella Thomas?"

"Yes. Good morning," Bella replied as she stood up and shook the hand that had been extended in welcome.

"Good morning. It's so nice to meet you. My name's Alison. Right this way, please."

Nineteen miles from Bella's location, local florist Ming Castlebrook winced. The petite thirty-two-year-old had been battling a massive headache all morning, and although she'd already taken something for it, the headache continued to get worse.

"Man," she muttered, eyes closed, an index finger rubbing soft circles against each temple.

Josie, her boss, glanced over at her and frowned.

"Still there, huh?"

"Yes," Ming replied, and grimaced. "But I can't leave. The Marshall wedding is this afternoon!"

"I know, but we've only got the bride's bouquet left to do," Josie reminded her with a shrug. "And they're coming to pick it all up, so, we don't even have to drive anywhere. Take the rest of today off, Ming. I can cover this, no problem."

"You sure?"

Josie reached out to take Ming's hand and squeeze it.

"I promise, I'm good. Now, are you at least feeling up to driving yourself home?"

Ming nodded. "Luckily, it's not too far."

"Then go. All I ask is that you text me that you got home safely. After that, take another pill and then go to bed," Josie advised.

A grateful Ming managed a wan smile before she went to clock out. She gathered up her purse and keys and stepped out the store's back door and into the alley where she'd parked her car. The bright sunshine tormented her already aching head, and she quickly slipped her sunglasses on in defense.

Thirteen minutes later, when she pulled into the driveway of the Euless, Texas home she shared with her husband Gary, she heaved a sigh of relief. The moment she was inside she dropped her purse and keys and made a beeline for the migraine medicine she'd been prescribed, took a pill with a small glass of water, then kicked off her shoes and climbed into bed.

And she sighed again.

Forgot to text Josie. Dammit.

Still in pain, and now frustrated with herself as well, Ming got up and walked back out into the living room long enough to text her boss as promised. Then she took a moment to text Gary too – he was out of town on a business trip, and she knew he'd worry if she missed their nightly call.

Massive headache. Came home from work, going to lie down. Love you – M.

Her tasks complete, she stumbled back down the hallway, stopping only to make sure her bedroom blinds were blocking out as much light as possible before she curled up on her left side, closed her eyes, and prayed for the medication to take effect quickly.

"Where are you headed off to?" Lizzie asked as she leaned against the open doorframe of Nathan's office.

"Meeting Bella for lunch," he said with a smile as he returned his cell phone back to the belt clip at his waist. "She just got out of her interview, and she sounds really happy."

"Oh yeah, that was today, wasn't it? With the publishing company, right? I hope it went well. She mentioned previously how much she was looking forward to that one."

"Yep. She told me just this morning that's the job she's most interested in."

"Well, you two have fun and tell her I said hello."

"Will do."

Lizzie retreated to her desk as Nathan left his office and made his way down the hall to the elevator. Within minutes he was stepping outside into the sunshine.

Nathan turned his head to the left, and smiled as he watched his wife approach.

"You got here quick! I'd have met you halfway," he offered before he leaned in and gave her a kiss.

"I walked really quickly," Bella explained in a breathless rush. "Nathan, I am so excited. I think I got the job!"

She tucked her arm through his.

"But how about we eat while I tell you all about it? I'm starving."

"Sounds good to me."

Two blocks down from his office, Nathan and Bella settled into a booth at Nana's Café, and Nathan's regular waitress approached.

"Agent Thomas! Good to see you. How's catching the bad guys going?"

"Slow today, Sherrie. But it's nice to have a break now and then. I'd like to introduce my wife, Bella. Bella, this is Sherrie, and she puts up with me and the team at least once a week."

"Nice to meet you," Bella said sincerely, and held out her hand. "Nathan raves about this place. I'm glad I get to try it out."

Sherrie beamed as she shook the hand she'd been offered.

"Nice to meet you too, dear. Now, I'm pretty sure I know what your husband's gonna order, but how about you? Want a menu?"

"No, ma'am, no need. He's gone on and on about the chicken fried steak here, so I'll have that, please."

Sherrie jotted the info down on her notepad.

"Okay, two chicken fried steak plates. And to drink?"

"Sweet tea," Bella and Nathan said in unison and made her smile.

"Ya'll are so cute together, by the way. Okay. I'll be right back with your drinks and some rolls."

Bella waited until Sherrie was out of earshot before she spoke.

"She's nice – and she reminds me a little bit of Jandy."

"I know, right? Me too. Well, Jandy and Mom combined. That's part of why I like coming here. Don't get me wrong, the food is fantastic. But it just... feels like *family* in this place. It's a nice break in the workday, for sure."

Bella reached across the table to take his hand.

"I love how sentimental you can be, my big bad agent," she teased lightly, and he squeezed her hand.

Nathan grinned.

"Okay, smarty pants," he said, and made her laugh. "Tell me about your interview."

"Well, I wasn't expecting to talk to four people all at once," she began, then paused when Sherrie appeared tableside with tall glasses of iced tea, two small plates, and a basket of warm, fresh rolls.

Bella closed her eyes and took in the aroma.

"Those rolls smell amazing."

"I make 'em fresh by hand every morning," Sherrie announced proudly. "Have been ever since I bought this place ten years ago."

Nathan's jaw dropped.

"You *own* Nana's Café?"

Sherrie put one hand on her hip and scowled at him.

"Why is that such a surprise?"

"I'm sorry, Sherrie, I didn't mean it like that," he backpedaled, turning red as Sherrie chortled with laughter.

She paused and winked at Bella, who was busy stifling giggles as she watched her husband try to recover from his awkward moment.

"Sorry, Agent Thomas, couldn't resist," Sherrie managed between chuckles. "Yeah, I own this place. I work the front of my house as a waitress because I *want* to. Gives me a chance to really get to know my customers. Besides, I've never been one to just stand around. It's a point of pride to be hands-on with my business."

She glanced toward the kitchen, then continued, "Speaking of, your meals should be done shortly. I'll be right back!"

"Oh, I like her, I really do," Bella announced as she watched Sherrie walk away before she grabbed a roll and spread butter across it.

"I had that coming," Nathan admitted sheepishly. "I didn't phrase it right at all."

"It's okay. She knew what you meant," Bella reassured him, and handed him the buttered roll.

"It's not just that. I've been eating here once a week for what, three years now? Maybe longer? And I've never bothered to learn more about her besides her name. How self-centered is that?"

"Fair point," Bella conceded. "But we've *all* had blinders on to others at one point or another. It wasn't malicious on your part, honey. And now that you realize it, you'll make an effort to look past the surface going forward. Take the lesson here and apply it."

Sherrie returned with their meals.

"Watch the plates, they're a little warm," she warned them as she set each plate down on the table in front of them.

"Thanks, Sherrie, this looks great," Bella told her, and Sherrie favored her with a warm smile before leaving them to their meal.

"Okay, so, about the interview," Bella began as she picked up her fork. "Like I said earlier, I wasn't expecting to be interviewed by a panel."

"What happened?"

"Well, the first guy immediately started talking to me in French. He and I spoke for a solid fifteen minutes, at least. Then the next person and I conversed in Russian. The third one spoke to me in German, and then we switched to English for the rest of the interview. Before I knew it, almost an hour had gone by. After that, they had me translate some written phrases into all three languages, then walked me around the place and introduced me to some of the other employees there."

"That's got to be a good sign," Nathan remarked, and Bella's eyes shone with happiness.

"I thought it was, too. They said I should hear something by next Wednesday, at the latest."

By two o'clock, Sugar Phillips' employer, Dr. Malone, had shifted from irritated to concerned. It was completely out of character for Sugar to miss work without so much as a text. Repeated attempts to reach her via cell phone had been unsuccessful.

"Someone should go over there," his office manager, Ms. Gillespie, chimed in. "I can swing by her apartment. She doesn't live that far away."

Malone nodded, and Gillespie hurried away to grab her keys so she could go check on their young staff member who was usually quite dependable.

Ninety minutes later, once she'd been cleared to leave the scene, a devastated Gillespie returned to the office and tearfully shared the news with her boss.

Sugar Phillips' remains arrived at the Tarrant County Coroner's office shortly after six in the afternoon.

After dinner, Donny and Jones both grimaced as Lizzie resumed her latest snacking ritual from the night before.

"I would never have come up with that combination in a million years," Jones remarked, his face twisted into a strange combination of amazement and disgust as he watched Lizzie dip another piece of black licorice into the mound of peanut butter on her plate, then pop it into her mouth with a sigh of contentment.

She shrugged.

"Evidently, I am not in charge here. The kid is," she replied with a wry grin. "And trust me, I know this is strange. I'm hoping that when the morning sickness finally stops, the weird cravings will too."

She glanced over at them both.

"And at that point, maybe I can get off the ginger tea and finally have a cup of coffee again."

Chapter Seven

Ming woke with a start a little after one o'clock in the morning. She rubbed her eyes, then sat up gingerly before slowly looking around her room.

My head still hurts, but not nearly as bad, she realized, and was grateful.

Her stomach rumbling as she stood up reminded her she'd missed both lunch and dinner.

"Hm. Shower first, or food?" she pondered aloud, and another loud grumble from her midsection answered the question for her.

She padded to the kitchen and stared blankly into the fridge for a moment before deciding to keep it simple – toast and a cheese omelet.

Ten minutes later, she perched on one end of her couch, her right leg tucked up underneath her, and ate while she scrolled for something interesting to watch on television.

Finding nothing that held her attention, she frowned, turned the TV off again, and focused on her food. Once she was done, she carried her plate and fork back to the kitchen and put them in the dishwasher.

"Well, now what?" she muttered to herself.

She debated grabbing one of the many books she owned, but she really wasn't in the mood to read, and while her headache had faded to a dull roar, it hadn't completely disappeared.

A hot bath sounds nice, Ming thought, and the thought surprised her. She rarely took one when a shower was much quicker and more efficient.

But the idea of soaking for a while was too much to resist, and she headed back down the darkened hallway to her room. She undressed, slipped on her plush, pale blue bathrobe, and went into her master bathroom.

She bent over to place the rubber stopper in the tub's drain, then turned on the water. Ming straightened up again to move to the bathroom sink and pull her long brown hair up into a messy bun – and shrieked when an arm suddenly circled her waist, pinning her slender frame at the same time a rag-covered hand clamped down tightly over her mouth and nose.

She struggled against her attacker, but at barely five feet tall and not even one hundred ten pounds, Ming was severely outmatched.

Once she was unconscious, her assailant removed her robe, then laid her down in the bathtub and turned the tap handles wide open.

It only took a few minutes for Ming Castlebrook to drown as her killer watched.

By six-thirty a.m. activity in the Thomas household was in full swing, Bella readying herself for a nine-thirty interview while Nathan prepared Charlie for the trip to day care.

"So, what's on your agenda today?" Nathan asked his sister as he and Charlie sat down with her in the living room.

"Well, I'm done wallowing in self-pity," Sarah announced. "So, I guess it's time to put a plan together, maybe reach out to some contacts? But first I need to figure out what area I want to target."

"Nothing at all wrong with staying right here in North Texas," Nathan pointed out with a grin as he tied Charlie's left shoelace. "And the rest of the family's here, so you'd have a support system in place, Sarah. I worried about you being out in California by yourself."

"Hey, I'm older than you! That's supposed to be *my* line," she teased.

"Nope, I've commandeered it, sorry," Nathan teased back as Charlie finally held his right foot still so his father could tie that shoe, too.

"Ready to go, buddy?"

"Yep! Bye Aunt Sarah!" Charlie exclaimed and raced toward the front door.

"Oh, to have even a *fraction* of his energy," Sarah remarked, and Nathan chuckled and nodded.

"You and me both, sis. You and me both."

Jerry Broder arrived at his office at seven a.m. on the dot. He detoured first to the breakroom to fill his coffee mug, then went to his office and logged in to his computer, where he sipped and frowned. Four more cases had been brought in after his departure Tuesday afternoon.

"Who's first today?" Isaac asked from the doorway.

Broder scanned the initial intake notes from the prior night's arrivals.

"None of them are marked priority, so, we'll take them in the order they came in," he told his assistant. "Starting with a Miss Phillips."

"I'll get her prepped, sir," Isaac assured him, and left Broder to enjoy his coffee in peace.

Hank arrived at the convention center at five minutes to eight, and as previously arranged, made his way to the coordinator's station to sign in and get his staff badge.

Here goes nothing, he thought to himself as he clipped the laminated rectangle to his breast pocket. As he walked, he glanced around at the setup, comparing the reality with the plans he'd made to not only keep Gabe safe, but to apprehend her stalker.

So far, so good, he confirmed as his eyes swept the main ballroom that was slated to house over one-third of the book fair's scheduled events.

Lizzie and Annie walked together to the eighth-floor breakroom around nine-thirty a.m.

"Still having to do the tea, huh?"

"Yes," a frowning Lizzie replied as she repeatedly dunked the bag in her mug and willed it to brew faster. "But hopefully not for much longer. How are things with you?"

"Same as always," Annie said. "Splitting my time between my desk and the lab. The techs are joking about adopting me again. Hey, you want to do lunch today? We haven't had an opportunity to catch up for a while now."

"I'd like that," Lizzie confirmed with a smile. "Fair warning, though – this kid has me eating some really strange stuff lately, so, don't be shocked at whatever I order."

Annie laughed at that remark.

"I bet. When my aunt was pregnant with my cousin she had some interesting meals for a while. Around noon?"

"Sounds great!"

"Two more, please," Mabel, her home health care aide, urged, and Sybil Rios Planchett groaned.

"Ugh. Do I have to?" she lamented.

"Do you want to get better?"

Sybil scowled.

"All right, fine."

She gripped her walker tightly and took two more steps.

"See? Knew you could do it," Mabel chirped happily.

Sybil's unexpected tumble down her front porch steps two months earlier had resulted in a fractured hip. Before then, she'd been a perfectly healthy sixty-seven-year-old retiree. But her accident had revealed advanced osteoporosis, and the former schoolteacher had been working hard to recover ever since.

"Okay, time for your medications," Mabel reminded her as Sybil eased herself down into the wheelchair again.

Once she was settled her therapist unlocked the wheels, then moved Sybil across the living room and into the kitchen of her spacious Benbrook home.

As she had twice a day every day for the last several weeks, Sybil swallowed the small group of pills – a single ibuprofen and some supplements - with a generous serving of water, then set the glass down on the table.

"What's next?" she asked Mabel, who checked her wristwatch.

"Well, I'll need to get lunch started soon, so for now, you've got some free time. Would you rather watch TV or read?"

Sybil arched an eyebrow.

"You already know the answer to this one."

Mabel laughed.

"Yes, I suppose I do," she answered as she wheeled Sybil down the hallway and into the space that Sybil's late husband had converted into a reading room for his bibliophile bride.

As she had every other time before, Sybil sighed with pleasure as she took in the custom, hand-built bookshelves lining the walls.

Henry had insisted on building her an oasis to feed her love of reading, and over the years she'd built up quite a collection.

I miss him, Sybil acknowledged, her eyes going misty with memories, until she was shaken out of her reverie by her companion asking, "Is there anything in particular you'd like to read today?"

Sybil smiled as she pondered the question.

"Let's see... choices, choices.... ooh, I know! Hand me that new Catherine Coulter book."

"Coming right up," Mabel responded with a grin as she retrieved it from its space on the second lowest shelf and handed it to her patient.

"Thanks, Mabel," Sybil said.

"You need anything else at the moment? If not, I'll start some laundry and then make lunch."

"How about a glass of iced tea?"

"Sure. I'll be right back."

Mabel returned a few minutes later with a tall glass that she placed on the side table beside Sybil's wheelchair.

"Have fun. I'll come get you when lunch is ready," she announced, then smiled and left Sybil to her reading.

Rick Connor appeared in Nathan's office doorway sporting a megawatt smile.

"I cracked it," he announced proudly. "The suspect's damn good with tech, but I'm better. Not only did I crack it, but I can also lead you guys straight to him once we get the green light for a full court press. I've already let the Director know so he can obtain the warrants."

"Nice work!" Nathan enthused. "Guess that means lunch is on you today?"

"Absolutely."

Jones was startled when his cell phone rang. He glanced at the screen, then smiled – it was the company he'd interviewed with only two days before.

His smile only got wider as he listened to Carl, the man he'd spoken with, formally offer him the position, and Jones wasted no time in accepting.

After a few more minutes spent discussing details, including his official start date, he thanked Carl, then disconnected.

"*Yes!*" he hissed, pumping his fist in the air.

"I take it that was good news?" Donny asked as he passed through the living room on his way to get more water.

"I got the job!" Jones exclaimed. "I start on the twentieth."

"Congrats! That's awesome."

"Thanks," Jones replied. "And I am so relieved it was the one in Pantego. I really didn't want to make that Dallas commute every day."

He clapped his hands together.

"So. Guess I'd better start looking for a place to live around here. Any suggestions?"

"There are some apartments only a few blocks from here, but I don't know a whole lot about them," Donny admitted. "Lizzie might be more helpful with this than I am."

"No worries! I'll ask her tonight. Speaking of – I'm gonna make a store trip. I'd like to celebrate tonight with a special meal."

He glanced over at Donny.

"If that's all right, of course."

"Perfectly fine with me," Donny said with a chuckle. "Excellent food *and* I get a break from cooking? I'm in."

"Cool! Be right back."

Still grinning, Jones grabbed his keys and headed out to his truck.

Frustrated, Broder sighed as he removed his gloves and other protective equipment, then pinched the bridge of his nose to try and calm himself. As they'd worked, it had become obvious to him that Sugar's untimely demise hadn't been a natural one.

"Nothing wrong with you," he murmured, more to himself than anyone else, and frowned as he looked down one last time at Sugar Phillips' face. "No good reason you should be here on my table, young lady."

"What do you think happened to her?" Isaac asked.

"Blood tests will confirm this, but at this point I believe her pump malfunctioned," Broder answered. "Make a call to the manufacturer of that insulin pump. You tell them I want the complete history on it, and I want it tested – *thoroughly* – and that they need to put a rush on it."

"Yes, sir," a solemn Isaac replied.

Broder turned on his heel and strode to his office to finalize his notes on the case.

By the time Bella returned home from her interview, Sarah Thomas had reached out to five different contacts and spoken in depth about the job markets each business acquaintance was familiar with.

She had to admit, it didn't sound promising.

Breathe, she reminded herself. *Just breathe.*

Sarah was suddenly overcome with the urge to bake something. *Lots* of somethings. It had always been her go-to stress reliever.

And 'stressed' is a severe understatement right now, she acknowledged.

She opened the notes app on her cell phone and began to look through the kitchen cupboards, building a list of ingredients she'd need for her endeavor.

Satisfied, she scooped up her purse and the keys to her rental car, then called out to Bella.

"Hey, I'm running to the store. Need anything?"

"Not that I can think of," Bella called back from her bedroom.

"Okay, I'll be back."

Fifteen minutes later a determined Sarah was standing in a grocery store aisle and scanning the shelf's contents. Flour, sugar, brown sugar, and vanilla extract were among the first items she added to her cart.

She could feel her shoulders becoming less tense as her cart began to fill, and by the time Sarah was in the checkout line, she was smiling.

<hr>

Mabel had been doing CPR for seven minutes when the paramedics arrived, but it felt more like an eternity.

She quickly moved out of their way and slumped back against the wall to catch her breath.

What the hell happened? Mabel's mind roared.

She had no answer. Other than brittle bones, Sybil Rios Planchett was in outstanding health – and she'd run the gauntlet of testing to prove it.

Mabel had only left her alone for fifty minutes. Fifty minutes. Same as every day for the last six weeks that she'd been Sybil's aide. Bathe and dress, a light breakfast, physical therapy, then reading time while Mabel cooked her a tasty and healthy lunch. Today was no different.

Except that when Mabel returned to Sybil's beloved reading room to take her to the kitchen for lunch, she'd walked in to find her slumped dangerously forward, the new book Sybil had been so excited about splayed carelessly face-down on the floor beside the chair.

She'd raced to Sybil's side and eased her back, only to find her unresponsive.

Acting on instinct, Mabel scrambled for the phone in her pocket and dialed nine-one-one, put the phone on speaker, and set it down so she'd have both hands free to maneuver Sybil out of the chair and to the floor as gently as possible.

She'd already checked for pulse and breathing and begun chest compressions when the operator asked the nature of the emergency.

Now she watched them work on the client that she'd also begun to think of as a friend, and her eyes welled.

Was it a heart attack? A stroke?

A worried and tearful Mabel honestly did not know.

Chapter Eight

"WHAT'S ALL THIS? Bella exclaimed when she walked into the kitchen and saw Sarah unloading several grocery bags.

"I'm making an almond torte and some cinnamon rolls," Sarah explained, then hesitated, and hunched her shoulders.

"Okay."

"And some cupcakes."

"All right."

"And a key lime pie."

Bella's eyebrows raised.

"O...kay...".

"I bake when I'm stressed."

"Oh. That's cool. Want some help? I'd like to learn how to make some of that stuff."

Sarah smiled.

"Absolutely! Where do you keep your measuring spoons?"

"Guess the kid's giving me a break," Lizzie said wryly as she scanned the menu, then ordered the chicken fried steak as she usually did. "No weird cravings – yet. The day's still young though."

"How are you feeling? Everything going all right other than the whole 'no coffee' thing?"

Lizzie sipped her iced tea then leaned back.

"Other than that, and the morning sickness, things are pretty good so far," she confirmed.

"When's your next appointment?"

"It's a couple of weeks out."

"Oh."

Lizzie looked across the table at Annie.

"How about you? You okay?"

"Well, no, not really," the younger woman confided. "I mean, I'm not bad, just... restless."

"About what?"

"Hank."

"Oh," Lizzie said, then frowned. "Wait, what? What's going on there?"

Annie filled her in.

"Um, yeah, you two definitely need to talk," Lizzie announced firmly. "Sooner rather than later."

Annie went pale.

"Look, I get the hesitation. Hell, it took Donny and me being put into protective custody together for us to finally face what was going on between the two of us. But that's not an option here, so, I strongly recommend bringing it up and not letting this go much longer at all."

Lizzie leaned forward, putting her elbows on the table.

"Because I can see it on your face, Annie. You're tying yourself in knots right now wondering 'what if'. The only way you're going to know for sure is to have that conversation, even if it's awkward. And you might not hear what you want to hear, but at least you'll finally know."

"Wonder why they're sitting over there," Nathan observed as he glanced across Nana's Café at Lizzie and Annie. "I know they saw us when they came in."

"My guess is girl talk," Rick responded as he reached for a roll. "Check out their expressions. Whatever it is, it's not a light conversation from the looks of things."

The emergency room's attending physician on shift didn't take long at all once he entered the triage room where Sybil Rios Planchett was still being treated.

"How long has she been down?"

"Thirty-two minutes."

The first-year resident rattled off the drugs that had already been administered, both at Sybil's house and at the emergency room.

"Defibrillator?"

"Three times already."

The attending stepped to the head of the gurney, glanced over at the monitors that displayed zero brain activity, and then checked Sybil's pupils for reaction to light.

"She's gone. Call it."

The resident stopped chest compressions and slumped his shoulders in defeat as he lifted his eyes to the clock on the wall.

"Time of death twelve-nineteen."

"It smells wonderful in here," Bella said as she watched Sarah carefully smooth cinnamon across the large flat rectangle of dough she'd made the hour before.

"I agree. How much time left on the torte?"

Bella glanced at the oven timer.

"Three more minutes."

"Excellent. Keep an eye on it. When the timer goes off, pull the torte out and set it over there," Sarah said, and pointed to an empty spot on the counter next to the two dozen cupcakes where a trivet was ready and waiting to be utilized.

Sarah finished spreading the cinnamon out evenly, then grabbed one long side of the rectangle and began to roll it up. She finished just as the timer dinged.

"Okay, the oven's empty," Bella announced.

"Great. Now lightly grease that nine-by-thirteen baking dish for the rolls while I cut them."

Sarah deftly sliced the cinnamon-laced dough, arranged the rolls in the baking dish, covered them with a warm towel, and set the dish next to the warm oven.

"Okay," she began as she washed and dried her hands. "Those need to rise for about an hour. While we're waiting we can put the pie together, and we can get the cupcakes frosted, too."

"You're on," Bella answered. "And can I just say you look really, really happy right now?"

"Really?"

"Yep. You're glowing. It's like you're in your element, Sarah. And I'll be honest here. I've never seen you like this anytime you've talked about marketing."

"What are you saying?"

"I'm saying, sometimes unexpected opportunities present themselves," Bella prodded. "Maybe losing your job in California wasn't the disaster it seemed to be. Maybe you've been presented with a chance to reinvent your career into something that brings you joy. That's all I'm saying."

"Huh," Sarah replied, her mind racing with the seed of an idea. "I'll think about it. In the meantime, let's get that pie started. Could you hand me a bowl?"

Gary Castlebrook pulled into the driveway of his home in Euless, parking his car next to Ming's Volkswagen Beetle. When he glanced toward the front door he was surprised to see his wife's boss standing on the front porch.

"Hey, Josie! How are you?" he called out as he retrieved his luggage from the back seat, then closed and locked the car door.

"Worried, Gary," she answered. "Ming went home yesterday with a really bad headache. She texted me and let me know she got here okay, but I haven't heard from her since. Have you talked to her?"

"No, not since yesterday morning," he replied as he hurried to his front door to unlock it. "I tried to call her before I got on the plane to let her know the trip got cut short, but she didn't answer. I just figured you guys had a busy day going at the shop."

He unlocked the door and Josie was by his side as they entered the house.

"Her car's here, and her purse and keys," he said, pointing out the items on the coffee table.

"Ming! Honey, I'm home. You all right?" Gary hollered as he swiftly crossed their living room en route to the master bedroom. Josie stayed in the living room, not wanting to intrude in case Ming was indisposed.

Moments later she heard Gary yell, "Josie! Call for help!"

Josie raced forward, following the direction his shout had come from, and stopped short in the bathroom doorway when she saw him lifting Ming out of the tub.

"Ming? *Ming*! Honey, open your eyes for me. Oh, God, baby, open your eyes!"

Josie fumbled for her phone and called emergency services as a crying, shouting Gary cradled his dead wife's body.

Sarah had been right; by the time they'd set the pie in the fridge to chill and frosted the last cupcake, the cinnamon rolls had doubled in size, filling the baking dish perfectly.

"How long do they need to bake?" Bella asked as she watched Sarah slide the pan into the oven.

"Twenty-four to twenty-seven minutes," Sarah answered as she set the timer, then turned to her sister-in-law and smiled.

"And now, we clean up while they're baking," she announced.

"None of that took very long at all. And if this stuff tastes even half as good as it smells, you could really have something here," Bella told her as they stood side-by-side at the kitchen's double sink.

Sarah shrugged as Bella handed her a mixing bowl to rinse and dry.

"I think I might go talk to Rick and Faith tonight. Thanks to you, I have an idea, but I'd like their input, too. Rick knows all about starting a business, and Faith's a wizard with numbers. It'd be good to get their take on what I'm planning."

Bella smiled.

"Well, I will happily volunteer to be a guinea pig and offer to taste whatever you feel like baking. Nathan will too, I'm sure. I don't know about Charlie, though. He's gotten better, but he's still a very picky eater. I constantly worry he's not getting enough vegetables."

Sarah grinned back.

"Challenge accepted. I bet I can come up with something that he will love and that is good for him, too."

Bella dried her hands as she glanced at the clock.

"Speaking of Charlie, I need to pick him up from daycare. I'll be back!"

Sarah watched her sister-in-law leave the kitchen, then looked around at the desserts they'd made.

I think Bella was on to something. I just need to line out some details first.

She retrieved her cell phone from its place in her purse, dialed and waited.

"Hey big sis," she said when Faith answered. "Is it all right if I come over tonight? I have something I need to get yours and Rick's feedback on."

It was a little after five p.m. when Broder and Isaac began their last autopsy of the day.

"Record on, please, Isaac," Broder directed with a yawn.

"Yes sir. Sybil Rios Planchett," came the response. "Sixty-seven-year-old Hispanic female. Cardiac arrest."

The case was documented thoroughly as they went along, noting liver temperature and other standard items that are part and parcel of a routine autopsy. The first surprise came once the chest cavity was opened.

Broder startled, and his gaze shot over to his assistant.

"That is *not* a damaged heart. Not from heart disease, at least," he pointed out. "Read me the notes in the file, please, Isaac."

"Found unresponsive by her home health care aide. The aide performed CPR for approximately seven minutes until the ambulance got there and then they took it over. Pronounced dead at John Peter Smith hospital at twelve-nineteen. But they noted her cause of death as *suspected* cardiac arrest. She made it here to us quickly, so....".

A look of confusion crossed Isaac's features as he stopped talking briefly and continued to read the chart sent with the body from the hospital.

"Yep, right here. The doctor that worked on her red-flagged her file and requested she be autopsied immediately."

"I see. And why did she have a home health care aide, exactly?"

Isaac skimmed further.

"She had surgery for a fractured left hip two months ago. And according to this, osteoporosis is the only thing wrong with her at all."

Broder's brows furrowed.

"An embolus maybe? Was she on any medication?"

"Supplements to help strengthen her bones, and ibuprofen, that's it. Might it have been a complication from her surgery?"

"Two months later? It's always possible, I suppose – but not likely," Broder retorted.

The coroner pondered the available data for a moment.

"I want a full blood workup on her," he decided. "Cardiac enzymes, CBC, chem 7, the works. And we'll have her stomach contents analyzed, as well."

"You don't think it was a heart attack," Isaac guessed.

The response was swift and emphatic.

"No. I don't," Broder answered immediately. "And the attending at JPS didn't either, from the sounds of it. My gut is screaming that this is *not* what it looks like, so, we'll need to run more tests than usual, please."

"You got it, boss."

The two went about their work solemnly, recording and collecting every single shred of evidence that might help them discover what really caused Sybil Rios Planchett's death.

"Hey Sarah! Nice to see you," Rick Connor said as he hugged his sister-in-law. "What brings you by?"

"An idea," she replied with a smile. "And I could really use yours and Faith's input."

"Happy to help! What's up?" he asked as they took the antique lift to the upstairs apartment where Faith was waiting.

"Well," Sarah answered, "For starters, I'd like you to tell me everything you know about launching a business."

He grinned.

"What did you have in mind?"

She held up the square plastic container she'd been holding in her left hand.

"You'll see."

Three hours after they'd begun, Broder stripped off his gloves and disposed of them in the hazardous waste container, then did the same with his surgical gown before he removed his headlamp and face shield.

"Mark all the samples as 'high priority', please," he instructed Isaac, who nodded.

"Already did, sir," Isaac acknowledged as he gently slid Sybil Planchett's remains back into her assigned refrigerated drawer and closed the door. "And I will hand-carry them over to Trish Wallace's lab on my way home."

The two men met over at the double sink.

"Good. Thank you, Isaac. I really appreciate your help these last few days. Hopefully, the others will be able to return to work soon and then you and I can have some room to breathe," Broder said as they both thoroughly scrubbed their hands and forearms, then toweled off.

"Amen to that, sir. Amen to that."

Isaac gathered up the samples that he'd already bagged and tagged for transport and left the autopsy suite. Broder followed, turning the lights off behind them as he went.

Chapter Nine

Lab Director Trish Wallace walked into the Tarrant County lab complex early Thursday morning to see Maribel, her lead tech from overnight shift, waiting for her next to her office door.

"What's up?"

"Several high-priority samples came in last night, and one of the results just doesn't make any sense. I was hoping you could look at it."

"Sure. Let me set my purse down and grab some coffee, and I'll be right there."

"Thanks, I appreciate it."

Intrigued, Trish hurried through her usual morning routine, swung by the breakroom for coffee, then headed down the hall to the laboratory.

"What have we got?"

Maribel moved off to one side and gestured at the terminal.

"See for yourself."

Trish perched on the high stool and scanned the results displayed onscreen.

"Whoa. That's showing almost twice the lethal limit! That can't be right."

"That's what I thought too, so I ran it again - and I got the same results."

"Interesting. We are sure the sample wasn't tainted?"

"As sure as I *can* be, given that I didn't collect them myself. But every sample was properly sealed. And all the other labs I've run so far have come back within normal tolerances."

"Any other samples that haven't been tested yet?"

"Yes. Stomach contents. I was about to do those next."

Trish reached out, picked up the handset of the phone sitting next to the computer, and dialed a four-digit number.

"Good morning," she said when the person she'd called picked up. "I think maybe we got a tainted sample. Can I send someone over to get another one? Okay, great, thanks."

She hung up and turned to look at the tech who'd brought the weird results to her attention.

"You up for a little stroll?'"

"Sure. Be back shortly," Maribel confirmed.

"Thanks. In the meantime, I'll get started on the stomach contents and see if anything pops."

As Faith and Rick worked side by side to make a light breakfast before their commutes, their conversation quickly turned to the previous night's visit from Sarah.

"I think it's a brilliant idea! She seems really fired up about this," he observed as he poured two cups of coffee and carried them to the table.

"She is," Faith agreed. "And I am excited for her. So much that I have an idea that I wanted to run by you."

Rick arched an eyebrow and busied himself buttering toast while Faith finished scrambling and plating the eggs.

"Do tell."

"Well," Faith began, "I was just mulling over what Sarah said last night, and it hit me. She could really use an investor to help her get it off the ground."

Rick leaned in and kissed her cheek.

"This is why we're perfect together, honey. Because I had the same exact thought myself."

"Great!" Faith exclaimed, then sighed as they sat down to eat.

"Now it's just a matter of getting her to set aside her pride long enough to let us help. She's stubborn. She'll be bound and determined to do it all on her own."

"Yeah, well, stubborn *does* seem to be a Thomas family trait," Rick teased.

"Ha ha, very funny," Faith retorted with a smirk. "Pass the pepper, please."

Annie Adams turned off the water, stepped out of the shower and reached for the towel rack. Her mind drifted as she wrapped a thick, oversized bath towel around her body and then wound a second, smaller towel around her hair.

After yet another restless night, she'd decided – it was way past time to have the conversation that she'd been avoiding for over a month. Armed with that determination, she'd worked up the courage to text Hank before fleeing into her shower stall.

Now she stood looking down at her bathroom counter, where her phone was showing a new text message notification - and her stomach was in knots.

She drew in a deep breath, then picked up her cell phone and pressed the button.

Below the *Hey we need to talk* text she'd sent to him was his three-word reply.

Yes. We do.

"Record on, please."

"Yes, sir."

Broder and his assistant Isaac waded into the first autopsy of what promised to be a very full day.

"Ming Castlebrook, thirty-two, Asian female, five-feet tall, one hundred three pounds. Preliminary cause of death appears to be drowning, which we will confirm upon further examination."

Broder paused his verbal observations, frowned, reached for a magnifying glass, and bent over at the waist, his nose almost touching the mottled surface of Ming's face.

"What do you see?" Isaac asked.

"Bruising. Bruising that is not consistent with drowning," Broder remarked. "Please read the file sent with her. Where was she found, exactly?"

"Drowned in her bathtub. Her husband came home and found her submerged and he pulled her out."

"Come take a look at this," Broder instructed, and Isaac hustled to the head of the table.

"See this? On either side of her mouth? That's from compression," Broder pointed out. "Possibly inflicted perimortem."

"This side here almost looks like finger marks, boss," Isaac replied as he gestured at the victim's left cheek.

"Let's have the lab run a full tox screen, too," Broder decided. "Just in case it turns out that she *didn't* have some sort of seizure disorder."

"Yes, sir."

Bella yawned as she walked into the kitchen, then smiled when she saw Sarah sitting at the table, typing furiously.

"You're up early," she observed.

"More like, I didn't go to sleep at all last night," Sarah confirmed as she tapped a couple more keys on her laptop, then flipped to a clean page to write another note down on her legal pad.

"At all?"

"Nope. I tried. I laid in bed for over an hour, but I was so excited I just couldn't fall asleep. So, I fired up my laptop and began to do some research."

She glanced up at her sister-in-law.

"Hey, you know this area pretty well, right?"

"I would say so, yes. Why?"

"Because I want to drive around and scope some stuff out in person before I go any further. Want to keep me company?"

"Sure! After I take Charlie to day care, that is."

"Great! I'm going to go shower, and I can be ready in about fifteen minutes."

"Take your time. I still need to make myself and Charlie some breakfast. Do you want any?"

"I'm good," Sarah decided. "More coffee and a hot shower are what I need the most."

"Suit yourself."

Sarah stood and stretched, then crossed the kitchen to refill her mug.

"Phase one is complete. Now on to phase two. I'll meet you back here," she said with a grin as she left the room.

By ten-forty-five a.m. lab director Trish Wallace was both surprised and concerned.

The additional blood samples that Maribel had drawn personally from Sybil Planchett revealed the exact same results as the first samples had — almost twice the lethal limit of digoxin, more commonly known as digitalis, in the victim's bloodstream.

That in and of itself had raised her eyebrows.

But what pushed her amazed curiosity over the edge into real worry were the preliminary results of Sybil's stomach contents. Here, the levels raised to thirty-eight milligrams – just under four times the lethal dose.

Trish sighed as she reached for the phone to call Broder.

"Hey," she said when his assistant Isaac answered. "Is Jerry around?"

"He's finishing up an autopsy right now. Need him to call you back?"

"As soon as possible, please, thanks."

She ended the call and continued updating her preliminary findings, and she'd almost finished when the Tarrant County coroner called her back.

"Jerry, I think we might have a problem," she said without preamble.

"What's up?"

"Sybil Planchett. Both her blood and stomach contents came back showing lethal doses of digitalis."

She could hear the coroner's gasp of surprise loud and clear over the phone.

"Seriously? But that doesn't track at all. Her heart was in pristine shape, Trish."

Trish sighed.

"I was afraid you'd say that. I think we'd better request her medical records, Jerry. Something is very wrong here. I'll send over my unofficial findings shortly."

"The typical medicinal dose in a standard treatment plan is between .0625 and a quarter milligram a day," Trish wrote in her case notes once she'd hung up. *"Therefore, it is my recommendation that the patient's full medical history be thoroughly examined as a means to explain how and why digoxin would be present."*

She finalized and then electronically signed off on the case notes before she forwarded it all to Jerry Broder.

One look at Broder was all it took for Isaac to realize that his boss had just been given some interesting news.

"What is it?"

Broder scrubbed his hands across his face in frustration, then gestured at his computer screen and announced, "It seems Sybil Planchett had massive doses of digoxin in her system."

"How massive?"

"Trish said twenty milligrams in the blood, and almost forty in the stomach."

Isaac frowned in realization.

"Forty? Good Lord. She would have had to take over a hundred pills to get to those levels. Are you saying it was an intentional overdose?"

"Anything I say right now would just be speculation. To definitively figure this out, we'll need her complete history. Get her primary physician on the phone, find out if she also saw any specialists, and pull as many of her medical records as you can, Isaac. And let them know it's urgent, please."

"On it, sir."

Annie sighed as she sat back down at her desk.

"Lab guys driving you nuts?" Lizzie asked from across the aisle.

"What?"

"Are the techs running you that ragged?"

"No, not at all. I like hanging out down there. I always learn something new with each visit."

"Then what gives?"

Annie's brows crinkled in confusion.

"I don't understand what you're asking me."

"Just checking on you. That was a big sigh a moment ago."

"I sighed? Really?"

"Really."

"Huh. Just a lot on my mind, I guess," Annie remarked as she typed in her passcode, then pulled up a file and began to scan its contents.

It was after four-thirty before Isaac was able to relay at least some of Sybil Planchett's medical information.

"I'm still waiting to find out if she was seeing any specialists, boss," he told Broder as he handed him some papers. "But according to her primary care physician, Sybil Planchett was never prescribed digitalis."

Broder's eyebrows raised as he scanned the documentation, then glanced up at his assistant.

"Then how in the hell did it get into her system?"

When Isaac started to answer, Broder waived him off.

"Rhetorical question. It was introduced into her environment somehow. No way to know if she knew about it, or if it was accidental or intentional. But I have an idea as to how we might find out," Broder announced, and reached for his desk phone.

A few moments later he was speaking with the chief of the Benbrook Police Department.

"Sully? Hey, it's Jerry Broder. Have you got a minute? I have something I need to run by you."

Ten minutes later, the coroner hung up the phone and looked over at Isaac.

"They're sending a team out to the Planchett residence to collect evidence. It should be in Trish's lab sometime tonight."

"Great! What's next?"

"First, I call her and give her a heads up, and then? Then, we wait. Any new arrivals?"

"Yes, sir, one. But I believe that case can keep until morning."

Broder smiled.

"Then it sounds like you and I get to leave on time today. I just need to make one more call first."

"I'll close down," Isaac offered, and Broder nodded his thanks as his assistant left the room.

The man he sought answered on the third ring.

"Thomas."

"Nathan, it's Jerry Broder. I have a case that I think you're going to want in on."

An intrigued Nathan Thomas leaned forward to pick up his pen once he'd heard the coroner's cryptic statement.

"What have you got?"

"A woman with zero history of heart disease who had damn near four times the lethal dose of digoxin in her stomach."

Nathan whistled low under his breath and grabbed a fresh notepad.

"Start from the top, please."

He furiously scribbled notes while Broder read him in.

"I take it they're going back to the scene to have a look around?"

"It's already in motion, and anything they find will go to Trish for testing."

Nathan paused.

"Okay, so, why call me? It sounds like maybe someone slipped her something."

"Because that's not my main concern now. I'm wondering if this could be more widespread than just this one case."

"But you won't know for sure until Trish runs her tests and finds the source," Nathan countered. "And even then, it could be an isolated incident. Angry family member, perhaps."

"Perhaps. But my gut says that is *not* what this is."

Nathan chuckled.

"Well," he conceded, "I *do* know what it's like to have a strong gut feeling about something."

"I know you do. That's why I called you. Just come see me, okay? Look at her case for yourself. Please?"

"Okay. I can be there in about an hour."

"Thanks, Nathan, I appreciate it."

Chapter Ten

One hour later, as Nathan pulled into a parking space at the Tarrant County coroner's office, several of Benbrook's finest arrived at the Planchett home. They were led by their chief, who had opted to personally oversee his team's evidence collection process.

As his crime scene techs began their search, the chief stood in the middle of Sybil's living room, speaking with the grieving daughter that had met them at the house and granted them access.

"And when is the last time you saw or spoke to your mother?" he asked.

"Yesterday morning," came the soft-spoken answer as she watched one team member head down the hall to her mother's bedroom. "I called to let her know I arrived safely at my conference up in Boston."

"How did she seem?"

"She was in good spirits. Laughing and chatting, as always."

"I see. And how much interaction have you had with her caretaker?"

"With Mabel?"

"Yes."

"I come see Mom three days a week when I'm not traveling, so, I'd say a lot."

"In your opinion, did they get along?"

Her attention snapped back to him, and her brows furrowed in response.

"Wait just a second. What are you implying here?"

He put his hands up in defense.

"I'm not implying anything, miss. I'm just asking some routine questions, that's all."

Now her eyebrows shot skyward.

"I don't think anything about this is routine – and I also think you know something you're not telling me."

"What makes you say that?"

"Because my dad died of a heart attack right here in this house seven years ago. I know for a fact that the police department's crime scene unit doesn't usually come to a heart attack victim's house. Unless there's something wrong."

She folded her arms across her chest.

"So, what's wrong? Why are you all here?"

He sighed and gestured toward the sofa.

"I think we'd better sit down, miss."

Confused and concerned, she took a seat.

"We've reason to believe your mother's death was not a natural one, so, we're here this evening to collect more evidence."

"*More* evidence? Wait. You mean....", she trailed off.

"This is an active investigation into her death, and until we find irrefutable evidence to prove otherwise, we're treating this case as a potential homicide."

She closed her eyes and shuddered.

"But who would do that? Who? Everyone loved Mom. Besides, she's been cooped up here in this house since her hip surgery. I'm the only one other than Mabel...".

Her voice began to shake, and her face paled as her eyes opened again, then went wide.

"Oh my God. I'm a suspect too, aren't I?"

"Thanks for coming," Broder said as he extended his hand to shake Nathan's.

"No problem. So, show me this case that's got you so worked up."

The coroner walked over to his computer, tapped a few keys, then gestured to the wall monitors.

"Help yourself."

Broder leaned back in his chair while Nathan moved to stand in front of the oversized screens to review the case documentation for Sybil Rios Planchett.

"Interesting."

"I thought so, too. And other than osteoporosis, her health was pristine. Hell, even her cholesterol levels were perfect. No reasonable explanation for the lab results we got at all."

"Homicide."

"Or suicide," Broder agreed. "But in my brain, homicide makes a lot more sense."

"Shoot me a copy of the file, please. And keep me posted on any further test results."

"Will do. Good night, Nathan."

Over in Pantego, Bella and Sarah worked together to prepare dinner while Charlie was occupied with a coloring book.

"I think I liked that third place the best," Sarah commented. "Those built-in glass display cases were gorgeous."

"They were," Bella agreed. "But I also thought that the last place we walked through was great, too. And it's on the corner, so you'd have more visibility for sure."

"Visibility for what?" Nathan asked as he strolled into the

kitchen and set his briefcase on the table before closing the distance to give Bella a kiss.

"My own business," Sarah confirmed, then smiled at Nathan's confused look.

"Sounds like I've missed some developments since you arrived on Sunday," he observed. "Want to catch me up?"

"She will - over dinner," Bella chimed in as she glanced at the oven timer. "The tetrazzini's done, just need to put the garlic bread in."

"Do I have time to make a call?" Nathan asked.

"Keep it short. We'll be eating within twenty minutes."

He grinned.

"I'll be right back."

He retrieved his briefcase and headed down the hall to his office. Not even a minute later, he had his boss, Steve Brown, on speaker phone.

"There's a case that was brought to my attention this afternoon," Nathan said as he removed his jacket and rolled up his shirt sleeves. "And if test results show what I think they will, we could have a big problem."

"Do tell."

Nathan recited the salient facts of Sybil Planchett's medical history and sudden demise.

"Christ. You think it could be another widespread tampering case, like back in the early eighties?"

"Man, I hope not," Nathan muttered, "but I think we need to have our resources activated and ready, just in case."

"I agree," Steve said solemnly. "Better safe than sorry. Keep me posted – and let me know how I can help."

Nathan disconnected the call and headed back toward the kitchen. But his journey was disrupted by the peal of the doorbell, and he altered his trajectory and opened the front door to reveal Rick and Faith standing on his porch.

"Hey you two! What brings you by?" he asked as he hugged

Faith.

"Dinner and conversation," Rick replied with a twinkle in his eye. "Bella called and invited us."

"Great! Come on in."

Nathan led the way back to the kitchen.

"Perfect timing, guys! I just pulled the garlic bread out of the oven," Bella announced, and smiled as Faith held up a bag.

"We brought salad. What serving bowl do you want me to use?"

Bella pointed toward the counter.

"Charlie, you ready to eat?" Nathan asked, and receiving a nod, helped his little boy into his booster seat as Bella clapped her hands together.

"Okay, so, it's buffet style tonight," she announced. "Load your plates and take a seat."

A few minutes later everyone was gathered at the table with food and drink. Bella glanced over at Sarah, who cleared her throat and began to speak.

"I have this massive idea," she said, "and it's exciting and terrifying all at the same time. But I want to tell you all about it. There are a lot of moving pieces to figure out, but I think it's a solid plan, and I'd like your feedback."

She paused and looked at Nathan.

"Bella and Rick and Faith have already heard some of this, but you haven't, so, I will start from the beginning."

"Go for it."

Her audience ate and listened as Sarah walked them through what she'd put together.

"You're going to need working capital," Nathan pointed out. "Do you have any estimates? Will you need special licensing? What about a business plan?"

Sarah's enthusiasm faltered.

"Not yet, but I am working on figuring all that out. I just wanted to wait on that stuff until I had chosen a location, at least."

She looked over at Nathan again.

"I think it's brilliant, Sarah," Faith interjected, frowning at Nathan before he could speak again. "And as far as working capital goes, Rick and I have a proposition for you."

After dinner Faith pulled Nathan to one side.

"What is *wrong* with you?" she hissed.

"Nothing. I'm just trying to make sure she's thought this through," he whispered back. "It's Sarah. Remember when she wanted to be a sheep farmer, even though she *hates* anything that is even remotely outdoorsy?"

"She was seven, for God's sake. What does that have to do with anything?"

"Look, I'm not trying to be an ass here. But she dreams big, always has, and when it doesn't work out, she gets her heart broken. And you know that, Faith. I just don't want to see that happen to her again."

Faith's hands fisted and landed squarely on her hips.

"She really wants this, and unlike the dream of being a sheep farmer, this one's attainable. And just for the record, Sarah's the one who talked us all down when you announced you were going into law enforcement. She had your back, one thousand percent. So a little support from you would be nice, Nathan."

With that, she stepped around him to return to the kitchen where Rick, Sarah, and Bella were brainstorming what Sarah would need to make her dream a reality. A chastened Nathan took a few deep breaths, then turned on his heel and followed.

"Sarah," he said as he sat down and took her hand, "I'm sorry if I didn't sound supportive earlier. But I am. You've got this, and I think you'll be brilliant at it."

"Really?" Sarah asked as her eyes began to well.

"Really truly," he replied and squeezed her hand. "And however we can help, we'd be honored if you would let us."

"Okay," she replied with a megawatt smile. "Okay, then. We have a lot to do to get this off the ground. Who here knows about zoning permits? Because I have no clue."

"I bet I can help with that," Rick offered.

It was almost ten o'clock before a Benbrook crime tech van pulled into the parking lot of the Tarrant County Crime lab. Three techs jumped out and began the process of carrying in a total of eight thirty-inch by twenty-inch by sixteen-inch plastic totes. Overnight shift leader Maribel met them at the intake desk, and her eyebrows raised as she observed the procession.

"We were told to focus on anything that could be ingested," the team lead remarked, then shrugged in response to Maribel's stare as he passed her a clipboard. "So, everything in the kitchen pantry, fridge, and freezer, plus some stuff from her bathroom. Figured we'd grab it all in one go. Sign here, please."

"Hey, I'm the only one here right now. Any chance you guys could help me lug all this stuff down the hall and into my lab?"

"Sure, why not."

Ten minutes later her visitors had departed, and Maribel was left with a plethora of evidence to wade through.

She looked at the totes stacked neatly to one side, then over at her workstation where her coffee mug sat empty.

"Yeah," she sighed to herself. "Gonna be a long night."

"Wow," Daisy, one of her co-workers, said as she walked in. "Where the hell did all *that* come from? Was I gone that long?"

"Planchett case," Maribel revealed, and sighed again.

"Jesus. Where should we start?"

"I have a plan but let me get some more coffee first before we get going. Are Brett and Devon back yet?"

"They were right behind me in line, so, they should be here any minute."

"Good. I'm headed for more caffeine. Be right back."

Within five minutes, the four of them were standing in the lab. Maribel reviewed Trish's notes regarding the victim's stomach contents as the other three stared at the totes.

"Stomach content analysis revealed the presence of twenty-two separate items," Maribel declared. "We will test as many samples for digoxin tonight as we can, and we'll leave the rest for day shift. But first, we need to pull those items to the front of the line."

Maribel read the list aloud and the team waded through totes looking for each thing mentioned.

"But which *type* of coffee creamer?" Brett asked. "Because there are three different bottles in here."

"And this tote over here is almost entirely vitamins and supplements," Devon called out.

"We'll test them all."

When all the desired items had been located, Devon spoke again.

"A lot of this first group are perishable items," he pointed out. "I'm going to grab a cart to transport them to the cold storage room and that way we can work each sample in turn without risking any degradation."

"Good call," Maribel responded. "Let's load up any other totes that contain stuff that needs to stay cold, too. With any luck, we'll strike gold with this first set."

Three totes wound up in the oversized walk-in refrigerator unit, and a fourth made its way into the deep freezer. Once that was accomplished, the team each grabbed one item from the pilot group and returned to the lab.

"Okay, guys, let's get started. Our mass spectrometer is gonna get a hell of a workout tonight."

Trish Wallace called a quick staff meeting at seven a.m. to bring her day shift staff up to speed.

"Maribel, walk us through last night, please," she indicated, and Maribel nodded.

"Eight totes' worth of evidence from Sybil Planchett's home arrived just before ten o'clock. We reviewed the stomach contents analysis and opted to focus first on the items found there. Twenty-two distinct results, but we have multiple containers of coffee creamer and vitamins, so, we wound up with fifty-seven initial items collected to test. We began the process of deriving usable samples of each item collected and prepping them for their turns through mass spectrometry. We managed to get four samples fully analyzed last night, and none of them showed any traces of digoxin. The fifth is running as we speak."

"Noted. The Planchett case just took precedence over everything else, people. Whatever else you're working on, set it aside. Ideally, we'll narrow down all these samples and find the culprit before the weekend's out. The moment something pops, I want to know about it, and I won't care what time it is. If I'm not here, call me. Understood?"

"Yes, ma'am," her employees said in unison.

"Good. Make me proud, guys. Find the source."

With that, Trish dismissed them. Maribel's team headed home to sleep while Maribel and the day shift traveled down the hallway and into the lab.

As Maribel went over her notes with the daytime shift leader, Trish retreated to her office and called Jerry Broder.

"No luck yet, and we've still got over fifty samples to wade through," she told him. "But it's our priority. As soon as we find out which item or items were contaminated, I will let you know."

"Plan to carbon copy Nathan Thomas on your findings," came the swift response. "Something tells me we'll wind up with his team on point."

"You don't think... Are you saying what I think you're saying? Do you think this could be another mass tampering?"

"Yeah. I'm afraid I do. I just hope I'm not right, Trish. God, I hope I am not right."

Trish's daytime team worked diligently and were able to successfully run another six samples through their sophisticated lab equipment through the course of the day.

And just like their overnight shift counterparts, each of them was disappointed when each of their six samples turned up zero trace of digoxin.

Maribel stopped in at Trish's office around four in the afternoon.

"You're here a little early," Trish observed.

"Yes. I was hoping we'd gotten a hit."

"Not yet."

Maribel frowned.

"In that case, I have an idea that could speed things along," she offered. "I should have thought of this last night, and I feel kind of stupid that it didn't occur to me sooner. I guess maybe I was overwhelmed at the sheer number of things they collected for analysis. That was the most I've personally ever seen from a single case."

Trish looked at Maribel over her reading glasses.

"Go on."

"Well, it occurred to me that we probably ought to test the most obvious items first, you know?"

"We are."

"Yes, I'm sorry. What I meant is, narrowing that tote of vitamins and supplements down further, if we can. Were there any partially dissolved tablets in her stomach? Were there any gelatin capsules?"

"I see what you're getting at. There was a partially dissolved ibuprofen and more than one gelatin capsule remnant. Wade through all those medicine bottles and pull out the ones that contain ibuprofen and gel capsules. Test those first."

"Yes, ma'am. On it."

Chapter Eleven

By four-thirty Friday afternoon, Steph Bronski had been reduced to alternately drumming her fingers on her desktop and squeezing her rainbow-colored stress ball as she waited for another service call to come in. The entire shift had been slow, and she was completely over it and ready to go the hell home and relax.

She glanced at the clock over on the far wall and sighed.

Half an hour to go.

"I like my job," the computer support specialist reminded herself under her breath, "but not when it's dead like this."

The subtle beep in her headset had her mouth curving into a grin.

"Finally! Something to do," Steph muttered just before she pressed a button to pick up the parked call.

"Good afternoon, and thanks for calling tech support. My name is Steph. How may I assist you today?"

She listened to him introduce himself and describe the issue as she typed notes into his customer record.

"Nice to meet you, sir. Okay, it sounds like I can help you better if I remote into your computer so I can see what's going on. Do I have your permission to do that?"

The caller agreed, and Steph's fingers flew across her keyboard as she walked him through how to download the client and install it and then give permission for both remote control and remote recording.

"Okay, thank you," she told him. "One moment please while I investigate this for you. May I place you on a brief hold?"

She pressed another button on her handset and began to explore the customer's setup to determine the reason for his technical difficulties. Within ninety seconds, she'd identified the issue that was preventing his financial planning software from successfully downloading the latest updates. Feeling triumphant, she clicked the button once more to take him off hold.

"Thanks so much for holding, sir. I've found your problem. You'll need to..."

Her voice trailed off as she heard an angry, "Hey!" followed first by what sounded like a crash, then by a distant gurgle.

"Sir? Can you hear me?"

But there was no response except another gurgle that reached deep down into her core and twisted her stomach into knots.

Turn on his camera and microphone, Steph's gut screamed.

It wasn't protocol; as a matter of fact, doing *anything* to a customer's computer outside of troubleshooting the specific issue at hand was completely against the rules.

But her instincts told her that for this call, it was vital, and rules be damned.

Hands trembling slightly, she remote-activated his system's webcam and built-in microphone – and immediately muted her own mike and opened a new chat window on her secondary screen to send an urgent message to her supervisor.

Call 911! she typed, marked it priority, hit 'send', and then watched as the gloved right hand of whoever had just cut her customer's throat from ear-to-ear wiped a bloody blade off on the dead man's sleeve before withdrawing from the camera's range.

Steph focused on her second monitor showing the customer account and typed furiously, determined to capture as much of the event on record as she possibly could, even as she fought back the overwhelming urge to be violently ill.

But a voice, so twisted and raspy with rage that Steph couldn't even tell if it was male or female, floated to her ears through the tenuous connection and pulled her attention back to the gory scene displayed on her primary screen.

"Demetrious Winger, your privileges have been revoked."

Steph watched and listened as what sounded like heavy footsteps grew more and more distant, then stopped after what sounded like a door closing.

She closed her eyes against the garish image still in plain view, exhaled slowly, and hung her head, trying to come to grips with what she'd just seen.

The hand that descended on her right shoulder made Steph scream and nearly jump out of her skin.

"Police are on the way. What's going on?" Brenda, her supervisor, asked, then gasped as she glanced at Steph's monitors.

"Oh... oh.... Oh my *God*," Brenda sputtered to the emergency services operator she was still on the phone with. "I think he's *dead*."

"What?" a stunned Nathan asked, and the unit secretary repeated herself.

"That's what I thought you said. Just wanted to make sure I heard you correctly. Put them through, Diane, thanks."

He removed the suit jacket he'd just put on, then reached over to log back into the computer that he'd just signed out of for the night.

Two rings later, he picked up his handset.

"Thomas."

"Hello, Agent Thomas. This is Detective Murphy with the Plano Police Department. We have a unique situation here that's gonna fall squarely under your jurisdiction anyway, so I figured I'd save us both time and go ahead and make contact."

"And that would be?"

"We have a murder with an online witness – and we have a recording of it. Well, part of it, anyway."

Nathan scrambled for his pad and pen.

"Walk me through it, please."

"A call came into a customer support center based up here in Plano. Someone slit the client's throat while he was on the call with the tech."

"I see. And the victim's location?"

"Grapevine, Texas, according to the tech he was speaking with. We're in the process of obtaining a copy of the entire service call, both audio and video. I'll be forwarding it as soon as I can."

"Grapevine PD looped in already?"

"They're en route to the guy's house. But I figured the sooner you guys get brought in, the better."

"Victim's address?"

The detective rattled it off.

"And the call center?"

Murphy shared that too, following up with, "Your eyewitness is a Steph Bronski."

"Thanks, Detective Murphy."

Nathan hung up the phone, shrugged his jacket back on, and raced out of his office toward the bullpen.

"We've got a hot one," he called out. "Lizzie, you're with me. Annie, take Rick with you to Plano. I'll text you the address. The witness is named Steph. You run the interview while Rick dives into the tech side."

"Will do, boss. You ready, Rick?"

"All set. Let's move."

As the quartet made their way toward the elevator, Nathan paused only long enough to dial Jerry Broder's cellphone number.

"Hey doc," he began. "Glad I caught you. Can you meet me in Grapevine?"

He listened a moment, then said, "Thanks, doc. I'll text the address now. See you there."

"What's going on?" Lizzie asked as they stepped into the elevator car.

"Some things you just have to see to believe, Liz," he muttered as his fingers flew across his phone's tiny keyboard to send the texts he'd just promised.

"Come on, spill. What's in Grapevine?"

"A murder victim."

"And what does Plano have to do with it?"

"Someone in Plano got an up close and personal view of it in real time."

"*Wow*," Rick and Annie said in unison.

"Yeah. That was my first thought, too."

The four of them exited the elevator in the parking garage. Annie and Rick turned right to head to his pickup, and Nathan and Lizzie veered left and strode toward Nathan's company car while he made one last call.

"Hey hon," he said when Bella answered. "Just caught a case. No idea when I'll be home tonight."

Lizzie followed suit with a quick heads-up text to Donny, then fastened her seat belt.

Nathan glanced at the dashboard's clock as he started his car.

"Five o'clock traffic," he muttered. "This ought to be fun."

Maribel's idea to narrow down the medications by pill type had helped – for the most part. Instead of every single bottle in the tote, she and her team were now able to focus their initial efforts on only nine of them, in addition to all the other things that Sybil Planchett's lab results had revealed as possible delivery methods.

"Mark the orange juice off the suspect list," Brett announced with a frown. "Nothing there."

"Can I run the sugar sample next? It's ready," Daisy offered, and Maribel nodded.

"Yes, and I'm just about done with preparing two more supplement samples," she said, "so we'll run those after yours, Daisy."

"Sounds like a plan."

A good seventy minutes after they'd left the parking garage, Nathan and Lizzie walked up the steps to greet the Grapevine Police Department personnel onsite.

"Good evening. I'm Agent Thomas, and this is Agent Zimmerman," Nathan said, and offered his hand to the lead detective standing in the front foyer.

"Nice to meet you. I'm Detective Morgan. Come on in. Plano PD reached out and said you were coming. We made it a point not to touch anything until the coroner arrived," the man replied, and shook hands with them both before he led them towards the living room. "And Dr. Broder got here about five minutes ago."

The trio stepped into an environment that had been carefully constructed. The home's owner had paired sleekly styled lines with a classic black-and-white color scheme, turning the space into a minimalist's dream. Along the far wall was a spacious chrome and glass workstation, with three monitors and other state-of-the-art components.

But the entire aesthetic was marred by copious spatters of blood - and by the very dead man being closely examined by the coroner.

Morgan pulled a small notepad from his pocket.

"Victim is Demetrious Winger, aged forty-six, divorced, lived alone. He worked from home as a certified financial planner. We're trying to track down next of kin."

Nathan jotted down his own notes as Morgan spoke.

"Thomas! You made it. Good. Come here, please," Broder instructed, and Nathan walked across the space to where Broder was putting away his thermometer.

"Liver temp consistent with the stated timeframe of events," the coroner remarked. "He died around four-forty this afternoon. And, I believe your killer was right-handed. He or she simply grabbed hold here," – he pointed a gloved finger at the victim's man-bun -

"and yanked the head straight back, then drew a very sharp, smooth blade from left to right across the exposed throat. From the marks, it seems there was a bit of hesitation at first, but oddly enough the wound is also quite deep. Much deeper than was needed to accomplish the task at hand."

Broder chuckled at Nathan's raised right eyebrow before he continued.

"My point is, the two are not congruent. Hesitation typically results in very *shallow* cuts. Whoever did this was nervous, at least at first, but something pushed them through it. Adrenaline, rage, any number of things."

He sighed.

"But it's your job to figure out motivation, Nathan, not mine. What I *can* tell you is that it took only about five seconds, perhaps less, for Mr. Winger here to exsanguinate to the point of losing consciousness."

Broder stepped back, peeled off his gloves, and looked over his shoulder at the two transport techs he'd brought along with him.

"Let them collect any trace and get their pictures first, please, then he can be loaded."

"Yes, Dr. Broder."

Nathan's cell phone ringing interrupted further discussion with the coroner.

"Thomas."

"It's Rick. The audio and video that Miss Bronski captured is *gold*, Nathan. They've made us a copy of the file and we're on our way back to the office now so we can start working on this piece."

"Please tell me we got lucky enough to get a look at the killer's face."

"No, unfortunately we didn't. But I'll start my analysis, see what I can get."

"Thanks. We'll meet you there."

Nathan hung up and glanced over at Detective Morgan.

"There's a security system here, right?"

"There is," Morgan confirmed. "But it wasn't armed."

"Thanks. Can we please pack up his computer so I can take it back to my tech guys? And route any trace evidence and copies of any pictures to the FBI lab also, please."

"Will do. Tom," Morgan called out to the lead crime scene tech. "Need to bag that entire setup for transport once pictures and trace collection is done."

"You got it, Detective."

"I hope like hell that this wasn't a random act," Lizzie muttered as she and Nathan made their way back out to Nathan's car to wait. "Because if it was, we have a huge problem."

"Agreed. Which is why you and I are going to drill down into Demetrious Winger's entire life story to help us figure that out."

As they climbed into the car Nathan clarified his statement.

"You take point on his financials and professional life. I'll take his personal life, including looking for any criminal history."

"Works for me. I can get the searches set up as soon as we get back."

"Do that, and then go home, Liz. We won't have many results to work with before morning, anyway."

"What, you don't think typing his name in will immediately turn up a giant neon arrow that says 'hey, here's your killer right here'?" Lizzie teased.

"That'd be nice, wouldn't it?" Nathan replied with a grin, then turned serious. "But no. My gut says we're gonna have to dig to find the truth here."

"Well, then. Set it up and leave, it is. Besides, I'm missing my snack time right now and my child is *not* happy about it."

"I'm scared to ask."

"Black licorice."

"Oh, well, that's not too bad."

"Dipped in peanut butter."

"Wait, what?"

"Yeah. Trust me, I know. I think it's 'ew', too."

<hr>

It was a little past ten p.m. when the focused quiet of the Tarrant County Crime lab was shattered with two simple yet powerful words.

"Holy shit."

Maribel scanned the results twice to make sure she'd read them correctly.

"What?" a startled Brett asked.

"The red clover supplement sample. It's coming up as foxglove," she revealed. "Dried foxglove leaves."

The four techs looked at one another.

"We need to run more samples on that bottle as soon as possible," Maribel announced. "How many more capsules are left in there?"

Devon shook them out into a small, rectangular metal tray.

"Forty-eight. But the label says fifty. And there's a second unopened bottle of them in this tote, as well."

He glanced in her direction.

"Do you think they were *all* tampered with?"

Maribel cocked her head to one side and considered.

"Tampered with – or substituted," she replied, her mind racing. "This test result shows *zero* red clover. Dammit. We can't run all these that quickly. We need more equipment."

She reached for the phone beside her terminal; her boss answered on the fourth ring.

"Trish, I'm so sorry if I woke you, but you're really going to want to come and see this for yourself."

Forty-five minutes later, after she'd conferred with both Nathan Thomas and Jerry Broder, Trish Wallace stood in the middle of her laboratory and rattled off very precise instructions.

"I want these two bottles packaged up very carefully and hand-carried to Dallas to the FBI lab along with a copy of your test results–*tonight.*"

"Yes, ma'am."

While Trish directed her team's activities in person, Nathan instructed his team via text message.

Nine a.m. tomorrow, conference room. We're now working two cases.

Chapter Twelve

NATHAN'S TEAM reassembled in the conference room on the eighth floor at nine a.m. Saturday morning. By that time, techs in the sixth-floor lab had successfully run twenty-four samples, thanks to the four mass spectrometers in their possession. At Nathan's request, Annie retrieved copies of the test results and brought them to the meeting.

"First order of business, the Winger case," Nathan began. "Grapevine PD found nothing wrong with the security system upon initial examination. It wasn't armed at the time of the murder."

"Or it was bypassed remotely," Rick chimed in. "I should be able to tell you that definitively, but to do that I need physical access to the system."

"We will coordinate with them to get you access. Now, fill us in on the recording that Steph Bronski made."

"I can do one better than that. I can show it to you," Rick replied, and crossed the room to pull down the wall screen.

He retook his seat and tapped a few keys on his laptop as Lizzie dimmed the overhead lights.

The file he'd queued up began to play. At first, the only visual was of Steph's computer screen as she remotely accessed Winger's system, but about three minutes in, the show became much more intense.

Annie gasped as the screen suddenly filled with a mortally wounded Demetrious Winger, his shocked, pale face twisting in agony as his left hand instinctively moved toward his ravaged throat.

"Freeze screen, please," Lizzie instructed suddenly as she stood up and moved to stand in front of the display.

"Check out the angle," she indicated, pointing at the gloved hand and forearm of the murderer in the still shot.

"I see it," Nathan murmured. "Killer was tall, so he or she reached downward and across to make the cut, not level or upward."

He looked at Lizzie.

"What do you think Winger's height was when seated like this?"

"Not sure but we can run some calculations and find out," she answered as she moved back to her chair to make a note.

"Let's continue," Nathan directed, and Rick resumed play.

Moments later they all heard the phrase that had further shocked their eyewitness.

"Demetrious Winger, your privileges have been revoked."

The video continued to play for several more moments before finally ending.

"Man... that voice," Annie managed. "Someone was *supremely* pissed."

"Have to be, to do that," Rick countered, and motioned toward the screen. "We need to wash the audio through analysis and see if we can't at least pinpoint whether it was a male or female voice."

"Not to mention – what privileges? Something about being a financial planner? Some club he belonged to? That phrase could mean anything," Lizzie muttered.

"Yep," Nathan agreed. "Which is why Lizzie and I will continue the task we started last night of finding out everything we can about our victim. Rick, you're on point regarding the electronics; we brought Winger's computer back with us. Annie, coordinate with our lab guys. They turn up any useful trace at all, we need to know as soon as possible."

He paused to take a sip of coffee.

"Now, on to the new case that has been sent to us. Sybil Rios Planchett, aged sixty-seven. It was originally thought she died of cardiac arrest, but evidence has come to light that speaks to murder."

He gestured to Annie.

"Initially, the routine testing done as part of the autopsy process turned up fatal levels of digoxin," she told the group. "However, Ms. Planchett was never prescribed digoxin; her heart was perfectly healthy, according to Dr. Broder. Further investigation led to two bottles of red clover supplements, among other things, being removed from the victim's home and brought in for testing."

Annie paused to skim the documents in front of her.

"*Wow.*"

"Wow, what?" Rick asked her.

"Sorry. Um, it says here that every single red clover pill tested so far – twenty-five of them – have all returned the same result. No red clover in them at all. They're all dried foxglove leaves."

At Rick's puzzled look, she explained.

"Digitalis – the common name for digoxin – is derived from the foxglove plant, the leaves in particular."

"Wow, indeed. So, what are we thinking?"

"We're thinking," Nathan said on a sigh, "that there's a possibility of mass tampering here that we need to rule in or out."

He looked over at Annie.

"Have all the samples tested so far come from the same bottle?"

Annie flipped through the pages.

"Yes. The one that was open already. Bottle A."

"Annie, you're on point on this one. Ask them to let us know when they start testing bottle B."

"They thought you might say that, so, they said to tell you they expect to get testing started on the second bottle by around six o'clock tonight."

"Good. If any of *those* pills return these same results, you'll need to get a battle plan together to test bottles from places *other* than Sybil Planchett's house."

Annie nodded solemnly.

"Will do. But I hope it doesn't come to that, Nathan."

"Me too, Annie. Me too."

"One more thing, Nathan. The lab guys also said to tell you that while the plant DNA database they can access isn't nearly as robust as any of the human DNA ones, they still might be able to confirm or rule out the source of the leaves if we find them a live plant to test."

"Really? That's good to know, thanks."

Nathan's cell phone rang, and he pulled it from his hip holster.

"Thomas."

"Morning, this is Chief Sully with Benbrook PD. I hear tell you guys got brought in on Sybil Rios Planchett's case."

"That's right, sir. The Tarrant County Crime Lab forwarded some items to us for testing."

"So I heard. I've located her caretaker, Mabel Potts, and she's agreed to come into the station for an interview. Thought you might like to sit in on it."

"Sure. When?"

"She's supposed to be here around ten-thirty."

"Yes, sir, I'll be there."

He'd no sooner hung up his phone than it rang again.

"Sorry, guys, one more minute," he told his team, and answered the call.

"Morning, Dr. Broder."

After a few minutes spent conversing with the coroner, Nathan sighed and disconnected the call.

"Broder just brought a third case to my attention," he shared. "A young woman killed by what was first thought to be a defective insulin pump. The manufacturer pushed it through priority testing at his request. They sent it back to him along with their findings. There's nothing wrong with the pump – as a matter of fact, the manufacturer confirmed that unit was *intentionally* programmed to deliver four lethal doses in quick succession about three hours before she died."

"I'm confused. Why would that land on our radar?" Annie asked.

"Because you have to have a passcode to be able to alter the programming. It's typically done by the manufacturer, or in a doctor's office. But they found evidence that the access code had been bypassed. The pump was hacked."

Nathan swung his gaze over to Rick and nodded as his brother-in-law stood up.

"Where do you need me to go first?"

"Broder's office in downtown Fort Worth to pick up that pump."

"On it. Let me get the audio analysis on the Winger video up and running right quick and then I'll go see the death doc. You have a point of contact for Grapevine PD? I might as well travel to Winger's house to look at his security setup when I get done with Broder, gather all my pieces today."

"The lead detective on scene was Morgan. I'll text you his number."

The team filed out of the conference room, and as Lizzie and Nathan walked side-by-side, Lizzie said, "I've got Winger's background checks under control. Sounds like you need to focus on foxglove leaves and insulin pumps."

"Yes, it does. And I appreciate it."

"So much for work being slow lately, huh."

"When it rains...," he answered solemnly as he pressed the 'down' button for the elevator, then stepped into the waiting car.

Lizzie veered off into the bullpen, sat at her desk, and called up the first of several search results for one Demetrious Alexander Winger.

"It *definitely* pours."

"Chief Sully, an Agent Thomas is here to see you."

"Thanks, Sarge, I'll be right there."

Sully, a tall, barrel-chested man, rose from behind his desk and walked with long strides toward the main reception area.

"Agent Thomas, thanks for coming," he boomed, one beefy hand outstretched in greeting. "Right this way."

He led Nathan down a long, light gray hallway before he stopped and gestured to a door on the left.

"Interview Two. She's in here."

The first thing Nathan noticed when he stepped into the room was the utter calm with which the woman seated at the table lifted her eyes upward to meet his.

"Ms. Potts, this is Agent Thomas," Sully said in introduction.

"Pleasure to meet you, Agent Thomas," she said in a rich, smooth alto, her face illuminated briefly by a warm smile.

She gazed in turn at each of the men as they took their seats across from her, and her radiant smile faded with each word as she continued to speak.

"I presume you're here to help find out what happened to my friend. Miss Sybil was my client, yes, but also my friend, and if her death was not natural then whoever caused it needs to pay."

"Yes, ma'am, that's why I am here."

"I understand that I am a suspect because I was the last one to see her alive," she said in a neutral tone. "I will answer any question you ask to the best of my ability and help in any way I can. For the record, I adored that woman, and wouldn't have harmed one single hair on her head."

She calmly clasped her hands in front of her on the table.

"So do what you need to do and ask what you need to ask. I won't be offended in the slightest. I have nothing to hide."

Thirty minutes later, as a tech worked to collect fingerprint samples from Mabel, Nathan and the chief excused themselves and stepped out into the hall, then into the adjacent observation room.

"I sensed no dishonesty from her, at all," Sully murmured as he glanced through the one-way mirror.

"I didn't, either," Nathan concurred. "I'm leaning toward a background check, just to be thorough, but other than that, my gut says she's not our killer."

He turned to face the chief.

"What's the setup out at Planchett's home? Any security measures in place?"

"Standard alarm system, is all."

"Hm," Nathan grunted. "I'd like a member of my team to have a look at it. He's quite good. If someone breached it, he'll know."

"I can have an officer meet your guy out there whenever he's ready. And Planchett's daughter is cooperating fully, said anytime we need to access the property, we can."

"Much appreciated. I'm also going to take a closer look at the grocery delivery service Mabel mentioned. Maybe that's how the tainted pills made it into the residence."

"I was barely out of high school when the crap hit the fan back in the eighties," Sully revealed. "But I remember the public panicking once news stations got hold of the story. I think that until we know for certain what's going on, we need to keep this quiet."

"Agreed. Shall we go back?"

At Sully's nod, they returned to Interview Room Two.

"Ms. Potts, we truly appreciate your coming in today. I'd like you to have this," Nathan said, and held out his business card. "If anything else comes to mind, please don't hesitate to reach out."

She took the card and nodded.

"I will."

As Sully escorted her back to the lobby, Nathan made a call.

"Don't just test the pills," he said when Annie answered. "Make sure they pull any fingerprints from the bottles as well."

"They've already done that," she assured him.

"Good. I've got a set that's been collected for comparison. I'm heading back to the office."

Next, he called Rick.

"What's your status?"

"Almost to Demetrious Winger's house. Why?"

"The Planchett home's security system needs reviewing as well."

"Okay. Meet you there a bit later?"

"Sure. Call me when you're done at Winger's place, and I'll arrange to get us access down in Benbrook."

"You got it."

Meanwhile, Faith, Bella, and Sarah sat at Bella's kitchen table and talked strategy.

"I've been mulling things over, and I've decided to put an offer in on that corner storefront," Sarah said. "The other place had those beautiful display cases already in place, but I just think the more visibility from the street, the better. Besides, it's not like I can't install similar cases once I can get in there and start renovations."

"Exactly my take on it," Bella replied before she stood and crossed the room to answer her cell phone.

Faith and Sarah grew quiet as she spoke.

"Hello? Yes, this is she... That's great news! I absolutely accept. What are the next steps? I see. Sure. Certainly. So, eight a.m. Monday morning then? Great! Thank you so much. I'll be there."

Bella hung up the phone and squealed.

"I got the translating job!"

"I thought you wouldn't hear from them until next week," a surprised Faith replied.

"I know, right? That's what they told me during the interview," Bella said. "And I certainly didn't expect to find out anything on a Saturday, either. But the office manager said just now that the managing partner *really* wants me to start on Monday, hence the call today to make the offer."

She returned to her seat with a megawatt smile firmly in place.

"Bella just landed her dream job, and I'm about to land mine, too," Sarah announced, "and I for one think that calls for a celebration."

"Absolutely! What did you have in mind?"

Chapter Thirteen

As Annie stepped into the elevator car and pressed the button for the sixth floor, she glanced at her watch.

Eleven-twenty.

She walked into the lab to check in and when she heard there were no test result updates for either case she was involved in, she nodded.

"Nathan's bringing in some fingerprints to compare in the Planchett case," she advised the lead tech. "I'm heading home for a while. Call me if you get anything."

"You mean you don't wanna camp out in here and wait?" he teased.

"Tempting, but, no," she teased back, then headed toward the elevator.

Within a half-hour Annie was unlocking her apartment's front door, and after glancing around at her still-bare walls, she opted to unpack more boxes and make her apartment look more like home until it was time to return to the lab.

She started with her two favorite pictures, already knowing exactly where she wanted them. She stepped backward into the middle of her living room and looked at what she'd hung up on either side of the bookshelf.

"Dammit," she grumbled when she noticed that the left-hand picture was about an inch and a half higher than the right.

Well, that's just gonna bug the hell out of me. Better fix it...

Sighing, she retrieved the tape measure that she hadn't bothered with previously from its place in her kitchen drawer. Returning to the living room, Annie placed one end on the carpet, holding it in place with her foot, ran the tape measure up the wall until she reached the bottom of the right-hand picture, and noted the measurement.

Then she moved to the left side of the bookcase, measured the same distance, and made a tiny pencil mark. A few moments later, after she'd rehung the second picture, she stepped back again, and was pleased to see the height variance had been corrected.

Her cell phone ringing drew her attention.

"Hey, Mom! What's up?"

"I am so excited, Annie!" her mother Mary gushed. "Your father just surprised me with tickets for a meet-and-greet with Gabe Crosson!"

"Really? That's awesome! Where?"

"Down there in Fort Worth. I'm kind of surprised you don't already know about it, as much as you love to read. Anyway, there's a great big book convention happening all week and the meet-and-greet is tomorrow afternoon. But John's packing an overnight bag for us as we speak, and we're driving down this afternoon. Gonna make a getaway of it."

"You're welcome to stay here, Mom," Annie immediately offered. "You and Dad can have my bedroom and I can take the couch."

"I appreciate it, dear, but he's already booked a hotel room for us that's within walking distance of the convention. But he *did* purchase three tickets for tomorrow, on the off chance that you'd like to go with us."

"I'd love that!" Annie answered. "Probably ought to plan to just meet you there, though. We've got a couple of active cases right now, and if there are any developments, I'll have to leave quickly."

"Fair enough, kiddo. See you tomorrow around two?"

"I'll try my best, Mom."

"Winger's system was remotely disabled," Rick said solemnly when he called Nathan back around noon.

"Are you sure?" Nathan asked before he could stop himself and winced when he heard Rick sigh in frustration.

"Positive – and when are you gonna stop asking me that? You already know the answer, or I wouldn't have called you yet. We wouldn't be talking. Now, you gonna listen, or what?"

"Sorry. Go ahead."

"Not only am I positive it was turned off by remote, I captured the hacker's IP address. Tracing back who it belongs to is coming up as a network-enabled coffeemaker, which is hilarious and which I know is bull, so, when I get back to the office I'll put one of my special search programs on it to ferret it out."

Rick paused.

"Unless you want me to go into the technical details at this point about *why* I think the result is bull."

"I'm good," Nathan hastily answered.

"I'll also need some time to dive into what happened with that insulin pump."

"Okay. Let me call Chief Sully and see when someone can meet us at Sybil Planchett's house. Can I call you back?"

"Sure. When you talk to him about arrival times, build in about ninety minutes for me to get back to the office and set up the new diagnostics."

"You got it."

"And Nathan?"

"Yes?"

"Lunch. You're buying."

"Deal."

Nathan hung up and glanced at Lizzie, who had just walked into his office with an update on Demetrious Winger's background search.

"You gotta stop asking him that," she teased. "You *know* he hates that."

"Force of habit," Nathan answered. "You know, measure twice, cut once, and so on."

He leaned forward in his chair, rested his arms on his desk, and changed topics.

"Find anything?"

"Bunch of nothing," she replied as she took a seat in one of his visitor's chairs. "Vanilla. No extraordinary income or spending, everything is right in line. No criminal record, either, not even a parking ticket. The only smudge that I could find on Demetrious Winger at all is an occasional library fine."

"So, nothing so far to indicate why he'd be a target," Nathan muttered as he ran a hand through his hair. "Dammit. I was hoping that digging in would reveal... I don't know... something, anything to elicit that kind of violence."

"So, the victim came back clean. That's not unusual, and we're far from done. We still need to look through his computer at his client files, browsing history, and whatever else," she pointed out. "We could still find something helpful."

He reached for his cell and dialed Rick.

"You on the way back?"

"Yeah, just pulled out of the drive. And just so you know, Winger had another laptop *and* a tablet in addition to his desktop computer. They're already in the back seat of my truck, next to the insulin pump," Rick revealed. "It made sense to grab them while I was there.

If the hacker got through his home security, there's nothing that says he or she didn't *also* hack Winger's electronic devices, so, I packed them up for deeper analysis. Kind of surprised you and Lizzie didn't grab them last night while you were here, to be honest."

"Didn't know he had them," Nathan told him. "The cops missed them in the prelim search, I guess. Where were they?"

"Stashed in a drawer in the master bedroom."

"What even made you think to look there?"

"A hunch – and good old-fashioned nosiness."

"Good catch. What do you want for lunch? We can order in."

"I don't believe that taking an *actual* lunch break at Nana's Café will permanently stall our investigations, do you? I'll be back to the office in a half-hour."

"Rick found more electronics," Nathan shared with Lizzie once he'd disconnected the call. "He's bringing them back with him."

Thirty-seven minutes later Rick walked into the smaller conference room on the eighth floor with a laptop, a tablet, and the insulin pump, all properly bagged and sealed.

Rick deftly reassembled the victim's primary computer's connections, hooking it up to the same three monitors that had been carried in from Winger's home the previous evening.

"Okay, let's get this rolling," Rick murmured as he connected one of his sophisticated laptops into the victim's tower then rapidly typed in commands and hit 'send'.

He pivoted, pulled his second laptop out, attached the insulin pump to it via USB cable, and repeated his launch commands. He then strolled to the end of the table where he'd previously set up the Winger audio analysis, and frowned when he saw it wasn't completed yet.

"Okay," he announced to Nathan and Lizzie. "Now, we wait. Hopefully by the time we get back from lunch, at least one of these will have something to show us, and then I can move on to checking out Winger's tablet and laptop. What time do we have to be in Benbrook?"

"We're not meeting at the Planchett house until four."

Rick grinned his approval as he clapped Nathan on the shoulder.

"Let's go eat, then, I'm starved."

As they started down the hall toward the elevator, Nathan remarked, "You know you're a hell of a one-man show when it comes to tech, right?"

Rick's grin morphed into a bright smile.

"I'm aware, but don't worry, I won't let it go to my head."

"Good to know."

Lizzie rolled her eyes at them both and smirked as she joined them for the ride down to the lobby.

Nathan's phone rang just as the elevator doors closed.

"Terrible reception in here," he muttered with a frown when he noticed it was Bella calling, then answered with, "Hey, honey, if you can hear me, I'm in the elevator right now, I will call you right back."

True to his word, the moment they reached the lobby he dialed his wife's number.

"Sorry about that," he said, then listened, and smiled.

"Really? Honey, that's awesome! When do you start?"

After a few more minutes he said, "Sure, that'll be fun. I love you too. See you this afternoon."

"She got the translating job," Lizzie guessed, and he nodded.

"Yep, and she's ecstatic," he confirmed. "They want her to start first thing Monday morning."

"Good for her!"

Nathan suddenly said, "Hey, I almost forgot to ask you guys. She wants to have a get together at our house on Memorial Day. Burgers and hot dogs on the grill. You guys in?"

"Sounds great," Rick answered.

"Is it okay if Jones comes too? He's still staying with us," Lizzie mentioned.

"Sure! The more the merrier."

"Cool! What do we need to bring?"

"Probably ought to ask Bella just to be safe, but I'm guessing whatever you like - as long as it isn't black licorice and peanut butter," Nathan quipped, then dodged her attempts to punch him in the upper arm.

"Sorry, Liz. I just couldn't resist."

The trio entered Nana's Café and were led to their usual table by Sherrie. After some joking small talk, orders were placed, and Sherrie bustled away to grab their drinks and a basket of the fresh rolls they were all so fond of.

They were almost done with their meals when the Director called.

"Good afternoon, sir," Nathan began, then faltered, his expression turning to a stone facade as he scrambled to retrieve his mini notebook from his shirt pocket.

"When?" was the only question he asked as he held up a hand to ward off questions from a curious Lizzie and Rick.

"We're on our way," he snapped, and scribbled down whatever the Director was saying.

He hung up and motioned Sherrie over to the table.

"We've got to go. Can I get the check?"

"Nathan, what's wrong?" Lizzie asked and noticed his brown eyes flashing with a soul-deep fury when he looked at her.

"Diane, our unit secretary," he ground out between clenched teeth. "She was attacked sometime this morning."

"You two go," Rick urged them. "I've got the check. I'll go back to the office and keep working on all the electronics angles, and I'll be in Benbrook at four as scheduled. It's all covered. Go check on her – and keep me posted."

"Thanks," Nathan managed. "You coming, Liz?"

"You bet your ass I am."

They made excellent time on the drive over, and by one-fifty, Nathan and Lizzie were striding into Harris Hospital via the emergency room entrance. The Director spotted them and closed the distance before they could even reach the intake desk.

"You got here quickly," he observed. "She's still in Triage Three. Follow me."

"What do we know?" Lizzie asked as they began to walk.

"Her daughter Mia found her around noon," came the crisp reply. "They were supposed to meet for brunch and Diane didn't show. Calls and texts went unreturned, so Mia went to her house and found her mother on the floor in the master bedroom. From the sounds of it, someone tried to strangle Diane to death, based on what Mia's told me so far."

He led them into a small waiting room just outside the triage wing.

"They paged Dr. Adamal, and he's in with them right now," he told them as they sat down. "They're not sure how long she went with her airway compromised."

"Long-term damage?" Nathan asked.

The Director shrugged, his eyes full of both anger and worry.

"They don't know yet. They need to run more tests."

The room filled with a heavy, palpable silence as they settled in to wait. It was broken abruptly several minutes later by the appearance of Mia and Dr. Adamal.

Lizzie stood and wrapped her arms around the obviously shaken nineteen-year-old, who clung to Lizzie and cried.

Chapter Fourteen

THE GROUP SAT QUIETLY until Lizzie was finally able to guide Mia to a chair, then sit beside her and take her hand.

"Here's what we know so far," Adamal began. "Ms. Mackinaw suffered a hypoxic brain injury. This occurs when the brain is starved for oxygen. Her injuries are consistent with manual strangulation — petechial hemorrhaging in both eyes, severe bruising around her throat, and a significant laryngeal injury based on the scans we've done so far. She also fought her attacker, based on the state of her hands and fingernails. We've collected trace already."

"What's her prognosis?" Nathan asked.

"She is currently stable, but critical," Adamal replied. "She's experienced some swelling in her brain because of the attack. The next step is to medically induce a coma for twenty-four to forty-eight hours and let her rest and hope that the swelling resolves on its own. But surgery might need to happen; I cannot rule out that possibility yet. I just don't know right now. We'll be moving her up to ICU and monitoring her very closely, and if anything changes, either my lead nurse Rebekah or I will let you know."

The neurosurgeon moved to crouch down in front of Mia.

"I know you're scared and worried," he told her. "But we will do our absolute best for her, all right?"

Mia nodded slowly, twin tears slowly streaking downward.

"Thank you," she whispered.

Dr. Adamal patted her hand, then stood again and left the room.

"He's the best," Lizzie reassured her, and Nathan chimed in as well.

"He took care of my wife Bella when she was in a really bad car wreck," he shared with the frightened young woman. "You couldn't ask for anyone better to take care of your mom."

"I just... I don't know what to do now," Mia admitted. "What do I do now?"

Nathan pulled out his notepad.

"Mia," he said gently. "Walk me through it. Tell me everything you can remember, okay? I know it's gonna be hard, but the more you can tell me about it, the better, so we can find whoever did this."

"Okay," she said, her voice quavering.

She took a deep breath, then released it slowly, and when she spoke again, it was with a steely, determined tone.

"Okay," Mia repeated as she dabbed at her eyes with the handkerchief the Director handed to her. "Yes. I'll tell you everything I can. Let's catch this asshole."

"It's not here," Lizzie announced just over two hours later as Nathan sighed heavily. "Which means the attacker took it with him."

The 'it' was the custom-made antique pendant necklace that Diane Mackinaw always wore. Mia had insisted that her mother didn't have it on when she found her.

"And she never takes it off. *Never*," Mia had stressed. "It was my great-grandmother's, and Mom wears it constantly, even to bed. So, if it's not in the apartment, then the asshole who did this to her took it."

At Mia's pleading, Nathan and Lizzie had agreed to personally search Diane's apartment for the necklace, and they had coordinated their arrival with Fort Worth Police's crime scene unit. While the techs scoured the entire place, collecting any evidence they could find, the two FBI agents focused solely on locating the missing necklace.

Coming up empty had them both frustrated as hell.

Meanwhile, Rick Conner had parked his truck and walked up to the front door of Sybil Planchett's home at five minutes to four. He was greeted by a uniformed officer and the victim's daughter.

"I'm sorry to intrude, but this shouldn't take me long," he told the woman, who let a wisp of a smile show before it faded back into grief.

"Take all the time you need," she said softly. "The control panel is right over there. I'll be in the kitchen."

Within twenty minutes, Rick's suspicions were confirmed. Sybil Planchett's security system had also been hacked.

He immediately called Nathan.

"Same MO as Winger," he revealed. "Possibly even the same IP address. Won't know for sure until I get back to the office."

"Come to the address I'm about to text you," he heard in reply. "I need you to test Diane Mackinaw's system too."

"How is she?"

"It's not good. I'll fill you in when you get here."

"On my way."

Annie had already checked in with the lab and was sitting at her desk when Nathan, Lizzie, and Rick finally returned to the office a little after six.

One look at the trio's faces had her own frowning in concern.

"What's going on?"

"Conference room. Lots to go over," Nathan instructed, and she stood and joined the procession down the hall.

The moment they were all seated Annie asked, "What the hell did I miss? Something big, by the looks on your faces."

"Diane Mackinaw's been hurt," Nathan replied, his jawline tense. "Someone attacked her, tried to choke her to death."

"Oh, my God," Annie exclaimed, her eyes filling. "What happened? Is she going to be okay?"

"She's alive. We won't know more than that for a couple of days, Annie. Dr. Adamal and his staff are taking care of her, but her injuries are...".

He trailed off, then cleared his throat.

"Like I said, we won't have a better sense of her prognosis for a day or two."

"Mia found her," Lizzie added quietly. "And obviously, she's pretty shaken up."

"Oh, God, that poor kid."

Everyone was silent for a moment.

"Anyway, not much that any of us here can do about that situation right now," Nathan said. "So, let's focus on what we *can* do. Annie. Any updates? What's the latest word from the lab?"

"I have a few updates for you," she said. "Regarding the Winger case, a few of the crime scene pictures clearly show a void in the blood spatter patterns. Looks like something was removed from his desk after the murder. But they only found Winger's prints on the entire workstation."

She opened one of the manila folders she'd brought with her, pulled out some eight-by-ten-inch color pictures, and handed them to Nathan.

"Now, on to the Planchett case. They started running the second bottle's contents about ten minutes ago. Every single pill in bottle A returned the same result – no red clover at all, only foxglove leaves."

"Not really unexpected at this point," Nathan reflected. "Anything else?"

"Yes. While the spectrometers were running, they used that time to compare the prints you brought in against those lifted from the bottles. No match."

She could tell by Nathan's expression that this news *was* unexpected.

"No match at all?"

"Nope. Unless she gloved up, Mabel Potts didn't lay one finger on those pill bottles. And there's more. Dr. Broder's office forwarded a set of the victim's prints too. Sybil Planchett's were all over that open bottle, and it also had three additional prints from unknown sources. But the second bottle? Three sets of unknowns - and none of the victim's prints at all."

"And they're sure?" Nathan asked.

"They ran them twice," Annie answered.

"Okay. Anything else?"

"Not yet. And I don't expect the first set of results from bottle B for the next few hours at least. It's the weekend, Nathan, so the lab is running a skeleton crew. Two techs instead of our usual six, so the sample prep time is much longer."

"Understood. In the meantime, start building a plan to expand your test sample pool if bottle B comes back tainted as well."

"You got it. I've already copied down the lot numbers from the pill bottles, and I had already planned to track down which stores in the area those lot numbers were shipped to. But the manufacturer's headquarters won't be open until eight a.m. Monday morning, so, I'll have to wait on that piece."

"Fair enough," Nathan said, and turned his attention to Rick.

"Any new data on the electronics?"

"Hopefully, I'll be able to share at least one update in the next five to ten minutes," Rick confirmed. "Give me just a moment to get the Planchett and Mackinaw data uploaded first, and then I need to check on the pump and the audio analysis. Maybe grab yourself some coffee?"

"I think I will," Nathan decided. "You want me to bring you some?"

"Sure, thanks."

When Nathan was gone, Rick looked over at Lizzie.

"Good to know I'm not the only one he asks that."

"I already told you that you weren't," she rejoined. "He asks *everybody* if they're sure when we're working a case. That's just how he's wired."

"It's still annoying."

Annie and Lizzie exchanged knowing looks.

"And we get that, but it is what it is," Annie told him. "Let it go, Rick. It's nothing personal."

When Nathan rejoined them a few minutes later, Rick took point on the conversation.

"Unfortunately, the voice analysis was inconclusive," he revealed. "No way to know for sure if it was a male or female speaking. The best chance we'll have to confirm that will be to get a sample from any suspects we detain for comparison."

"That is unfortunate," Nathan agreed. "What about the other diagnostics?"

"Well, so far, the IP address involved in taking Winger's home security system offline and altering Sugar Phillips' insulin doses are one and the same," Rick answered. "I'm cross-checking the data dumps from the Planchett and Mackinaw systems as we speak. Should know something within an hour, ninety minutes, tops."

He leaned back in his chair and crossed his arms.

"And I've been trying to trace the IP address to its source, but it's bounced all over the place," he said, frowning. "Whoever this person is, they're really, really good."

"Like *how* good?"

"Like, 'Second World government or mid-level hacker' good,"

Rick confirmed. "Not infallible, mind you, just very good at covering their tracks. But I'll find them, you can count on it."

He swiveled his head to look at Nathan.

"And yes, before you ask – I'm sure."

Nathan smiled.

"Okay, then. Anything else we can accomplish tonight, folks?"

"I don't think so," Annie chimed in. "I mean, it's gonna take the lab a while to get through all fifty pills in that bottle. Figure ninety minutes per sample, on average. Even with all four machines running, we're still looking at some time tomorrow before it's all completed."

"Other than continuing to wade into Winger's business records, there's not a lot to do right now on that case, either," Lizzie told the group. "Physical evidence has been collected and is being analyzed. Right now, there's nothing left to chase; we're in a holding pattern until something we can work with turns up."

"Agreed," Rick said. "I mean, we know so far that two of the four cases were likely committed by the same person or people, but are there any other commonalities?"

"No," Nathan answered on a heavy exhale. "Race, gender, age, marital status, occupation, all differ. These people have nothing in common at all that we know of."

Rick's computer chiming disrupted the conversation, and he hustled to the end of the table.

"It's official," he said as he looked at his team members. "The same IP address was used in all four of these cases. Now I just need to track it to the source."

"Okay. Rick, keep working on that piece. As far as the rest of us goes - that's where we start first thing on Monday if we don't get any new pieces to work with before then. We'll reach out to the supplement manufacturer, and we'll cross-check each victim's background. There's got to be something else tying these people together besides that IP address. We just have to figure out what it is."

"So then let's split it out. Divide and conquer," Lizzie suggested. "I'll keep going on Winger."

"I'll take Sybil Planchett," Annie offered.

"I'll work on Sugar Phillips," Rick said. "I need something else to do while my tracker is running."

"And I will find out more about Diane," Nathan murmured. "I just hope she'll understand when she finds out I'm digging into her personal life."

"If it helps find out who hurt her, I'm sure she will," Lizzie told him earnestly.

"It's settled, then. We'll meet here in the conference room Monday afternoon and compare everything we've found at that point," Nathan announced as he stood up.

"Now. It's been a very full Saturday for all of us. I want each of you to take tomorrow off and rest up, guys, because it could be our last day off for a while," he advised his team. "We're going to hit the ground running Monday morning."

With that, the group disbanded, and Lizzie waited until Rick and Annie had left the room before she followed her instinct and asked the question.

"You're taking off tomorrow too, right?"

"I figured I might go ahead and start..." Nathan began but was stopped mid-sentence.

"*Nope*," Lizzie told him sternly. "*You* need to walk away from all this for a day, too. Spend tomorrow with Bella and Charlie. Promise me."

Her eyebrow arched when she noticed his stubborn glare.

"Uh, no. Don't give me that look – and don't get me started. You need to take breaks too, Nathan, just like the rest of us do. Besides, you and I both know that there probably won't even be an update on Diane's condition before Monday anyway. Right?"

It was a battle of wills as much as a staring contest, and she crossed her arms and leaned back against the table, determined to wait him out.

"God, you're even more pig-headed than usual, Liz!" he said playfully.

"Takes one to know one," she fired right back.

He grinned.

"All right, fine," he finally said with a laugh as he added folders to his briefcase.

"Fine," she echoed, then smirked. "Glad you caved – you were about to make me miss my snack time! See you on Monday."

She could still hear Nathan chuckling behind her as she headed toward the elevator.

———

Nathan arrived home around seven-twenty and was immediately greeted by a very enthusiastic Charlie.

"Hi Daddy!" he shrieked, arms outstretched so that Nathan could pick him up.

"Hey, buddy! How was your day?"

"Good!" the little boy exclaimed. "Missed you."

"I missed you too," Nathan told him. "Let's go find Mom, shall we?"

They walked into the kitchen where Bella had just made herself a cup of tea.

"Hey, honey, sorry I was gone so long today," he told Bella before leaning in for a kiss. "So, tell me about the phone call! What did they say?"

"Happy to fill you in – if you sit down and let me make you a plate right quick," she responded. "I kept dinner warm for you. You look tired."

"I'm all right," he answered as he took a seat with Charlie balanced on his lap. "It's just that what we thought were three separate cases all seem to have dovetailed together. And Diane got hurt."

"Oh no! What happened?"

He glanced down at Charlie.

"I'll tell you what I can during soak time. Deal?"

"Deal," she agreed, and set his plate on the table before she sat down next to him and sipped her tea.

"Thanks," he said. "Hey, where's Sarah?"

"At Faith's," he was told by a grinning Bella. "Sarah's so excited it's almost contagious, and I think Faith might even be more excited than Sarah, if you can believe that. Between the two of them, 'Operation Fulfill the Dream' is rapidly gaining ground. Among other things, Sarah got hold of the realtor and made a formal offer on the retail space she wants."

"Nice! Now, tell me about the call you got."

Chapter Fifteen

Nathan yawned as he shuffled toward the kitchen to get the coffeepot started on Sunday morning.

His sleep had been spotty. Although he'd gone to bed at a decent hour, his subconscious arranging and rearranging the puzzle pieces of what the team had learned so far about all four cases had made it difficult for him to fall asleep quickly. He'd stared at the ceiling fan, his mind churning, until he'd finally drifted off sometime in the wee hours of the morning.

He'd awakened suddenly just before six o'clock, startled into awareness by a wisp of a thought that now refused to cooperate and show itself to him for closer inspection.

Nathan flipped on the light switch before he crossed the kitchen to pour his usual measure of coffee grounds into the coffeemaker's basket. He picked up the empty pot, pivoted to the sink to fill it with water, then poured the water into the machine and set the pot back into position. He yawned again as he pressed the power button and grabbed a mug from the nearest cabinet.

He stood, still bleary-eyed, watching the machine slowly start to brew his much-needed beverage, and almost shouted when Bella's hand touched his shoulder.

"God," he managed as he whirled around. "What are you doing up?"

She smiled.

"I'm not sure. Especially this early on a Sunday. Why are *you* up?"

"I'm still running over case stuff in my head," he confessed. "Took me forever to get to sleep last night."

"I thought you told your team to take today off?" she asked as she maneuvered past him to add water to the teakettle, set it on the stove, and turn on the burner.

"I did."

"Okay, so, shouldn't you take your own advice? We could have a family day. What do you think about packing up a picnic lunch and taking Charlie to the Fort Worth zoo?"

"I like that idea," Nathan confirmed.

She walked back over to him and wrapped her arms around his waist.

"Besides," she said softly, "you and I both know that stepping away from what you're working on for a while isn't a bad thing at all. It allows you to come back to it with a fresh perspective. And from the little you were able to share with me last night, it sounds like things are in a holding pattern until tomorrow anyway. So, you might as well spend some time with me and Charlie out in the sunshine. Right?"

"Right," Nathan agreed.

He leaned down for a kiss, then rested his chin on the top of her head. They stood in the center of their kitchen, content to simply enjoy each other and their quiet, calm Sunday morning.

"Your coffee's ready," she pointed out after a few minutes, and she stepped out of his embrace to tend to the whistling teakettle on the stove while he poured himself his first caffeine-filled cup of the day.

"Speaking of family day, I think I'll get started on making break-fast for us once I finish my coffee. What sounds better with blueberry pancakes – bacon, or sausage?"

Bella smiled at him as she dunked her tea bag into her mug of hot water.

"I'm good with either one, so, cook's choice. Surprise me."

Hank Myers' alarm pealed to life at seven o'clock sharp and he immediately reached out to swat it into silence; he'd already been wide awake for the past half-hour.

This is it, he acknowledged. *The last day, and our best chance to catch whoever is after Gabe.*

And the day's logistics already had him on edge.

The book fair had been packed with people all week long; the first two presentations Gabe had given had been filled almost to over-flowing with authors eager to hear her speak.

He hadn't realized at first that Sunday's session wasn't just open to the public – it was ending with an up-close and personal meet-and-greet session with Gabe's fans. Short of his co-workers hovering on all sides of her the entire time, Hank had serious concerns about Gabe's safety in that situation.

He'd immediately reached out to Allen and voiced his concerns, who assured him that the team members acting as her personal secu-rity for the event would indeed be within arm's reach of her throughout the meet-and-greet portion.

Which left only her time standing alone at the podium for roughly the first forty minutes of the session to worry about...

Hank sighed as he threw back the covers, stood, and headed for the shower. Twenty minutes later he was putting on his jeans, socks, and shoes and contemplating whether Annie was awake.

I should at least text her and make dinner plans for tomorrow night, he thought to himself, and felt guilty that other than a three-word response he hadn't reached out to her since Thursday.

Then again, he realized, she *hasn't made contact, either…*

And none of that matters right now. Not until Gabe is safe. Focus. There's a lot riding on you.

He sighed again as he started to stay on task and go to his closet to grab a shirt but found himself diverting to pick up his cell phone and fire off a quick message to the woman he couldn't get out of his mind.

"There," he announced to his empty room as he resumed his morning routine. "*Now* maybe I can focus."

"Feel like doing anything today?" Donny asked her as they sat down for breakfast around eight-fifteen.

"What did you have in mind?" Lizzie responded as she spread cream cheese on a warm bagel.

He shrugged.

"Oh, I bet we could figure something out," he replied with a grin. "Walk around over in Sundance Square, for starters, or go check out the gardens, maybe?"

Her brow furrowed.

"Gardens?"

"The Botanical Gardens," he prompted. "I was born and raised here, but I've never been to see them. I hear they're beautiful."

"I haven't either," she confided. "Yeah, that sounds like fun! And maybe at some point today we could check out some baby stuff, too."

"We've got lots of time for that still," he pointed out.

"I know it *seems* that way, but I'm already almost done with the first trimester," Lizzie reminded him. "And it feels like just yesterday that we even found out I was pregnant. I just really think we ought to start shopping for baby stuff while I can still get around easily. If we wait too long, who knows? I might get so big with this kid that I can barely walk."

"You have a good point."

"Besides, when have you known me to actually *want* to go shopping for anything at all besides groceries?"

"Touché," Donny said with a smirk.

"Right. So, humor me. The gardens first, before it gets too hot, and then baby stuff."

"You got it."

"And maybe ice cream mixed in there somewhere?"

"And lunch too, absolutely."

"Cool!" she exclaimed and took a bite of her bagel.

Once she swallowed it she said, "Now, tell me about Jones' new place. You told him he could stay here for as long as he needed to, right?"

"I did, and he wouldn't listen. Said that he really appreciated the offer, but that he'd inconvenienced us long enough."

"Oh, whatever," Lizzie said dismissively, and Donny chuckled.

"I'm just telling you what he said."

"I know. I just wanted to make sure he didn't feel pressured to hurry up and get his own place. It's almost weird he's leaving already."

"Meaning?"

She shrugged.

"I don't know how to explain it, exactly."

Donny leaned in close.

"I have a confession to make," he said solemnly, and Lizzie's eyes sparkled.

"Do tell."

"I was kinda getting spoiled, with him cooking dinner so often."

She laughed and nodded.

They finished their breakfast in silence until Lizzie gasped.

"Oh, no. I forgot to tell Jones!"

"Tell Jones what?"

"That he's invited to come with us to Nathan's on Memorial Day!

I just assumed that he'd still be staying here with us by next weekend, so I forgot to mention it."

Donny reached over and squeezed her hand.

"No worries. I did tell him, and *he* said to tell *you* that he'll be there."

"Good, thanks," she said as she stood and carried her plate over to the dishwasher. "Now. You ready to go see some gardens?"

Over in her apartment in Irving, Annie yawned and stretched, then exhaled slowly as she turned her head to glance at the clock on her bedside table.

Almost nine already? I hardly ever sleep this late.

She languidly rose to her feet, then stretched again before she padded across the thick, plush carpet to the bathroom.

Mom said to meet them at two, she recalled as she reached for the shower faucet. *But maybe we can grab lunch before we go to the book fair.*

Annie hustled out to the kitchen to retrieve her cell phone from its charger, her sole intention to text her parents and arrange a meal together.

She stopped dead in her tracks when she noticed a new text message from Hank.

Hey there. I miss you. Can we grab dinner tomorrow night and talk?

Her current course of action temporarily forgotten, Annie beamed as she messaged him back.

I'd like that. Seven o'clock?

Hank paused outside the main entrance of the book fair when his phone buzzed, and he smiled when he saw Annie had accepted his impromptu dinner invitation.

He quickly texted her back, then tucked his phone away and walked through the automatic double doors, his game face on, his senses shifting to high alert.

Mere seconds after Annie hit 'send', her phone chirped with his reply.

Perfect. I'll pick you up?

Great. See you then, she responded, still smiling as she switched gears and dialed her mother's number.

"Hey, Mom. You guys want to have lunch before we go to the book fair? There's a great sandwich place called Milo's a couple of blocks down from there."

"What time?"

"Eleven-thirty? That way we can get in and get out before the lunch crowd rolls through."

"You bet."

Satisfied, Annie set her phone down and resumed her trip to the shower to get ready for her day.

By the time Annie met her parents for lunch at eleven-thirty, Nathan, Bella, and Charlie had already visited the rhino, elephant, lion, and giraffe exhibits.

A visibly excited Charlie tugged his parents' hands.

"Monkeys! Let's go see the monkeys! And then the meerkats!"

"Okay, buddy, relax," Bella answered him with a laugh. "I promise you they're not going to disappear before we get there."

"And we also need to eat lunch, buddy," Nathan reminded his son. "Are you hungry yet?"

"Mac and cheese?"

"Sandwiches," Nathan told him, and tried to keep his own expression neutral when Charlie's scrunched into a scowl. "Mac and cheese isn't really a good picnic food."

"Why?"

"Because sandwiches are less messy on a picnic, Charlie," Bella chimed in.

"Okay," Charlie replied, mollified by the logic. "But can we have peanut butter and jelly?"

"Yes," he was assured by his mother. "And chips and a juice box."

"Yay!"

"Nice save," Nathan whispered to her.

"Thanks," Bella whispered back.

"I didn't realize the gardens were so big," Lizzie lamented as she buckled her seat belt. "We didn't even get halfway through them."

"Well, that just means we can come back another time and do more exploring," Donny answered.

"When it's autumn, that is," he amended as he turned the ignition key and savored the cool air blowing on them both from his truck's vents.

"I don't know about you, Liz, but I think I got too used to living in Vail. In my opinion, it's *already* too hot to spend much more time outside today."

"Agreed. The average temperature in Seattle this time of year is usually below seventy degrees. So, I vote for lunch and ice cream time. How about Milo's?"

"Sounds like a plan," he agreed. "And after that, maybe we can start the shopping part of our day at the mall? Lots of stores to choose from, and all the walking is *inside*."

"I bet we can make that work. Food first, though, I'm starving," she told him with a grin.

—

Ten minutes later Donny held the restaurant's door open for her, then followed her in to wait at the hostess stand.

"It's a little crowded already," Lizzie observed before a waving hand across the space caught her attention.

"Hey, look! Annie's here," she said, and waved back.

When Annie motioned for them to join her, Lizzie glanced at the hostess.

"We'd like to sit with them," she said, and pointed across the space.

"Sure, go right ahead."

Donny and Lizzie wove their way around patron-filled tables until they reached the rectangular one where Annie and two other people were seated.

"Hey, guys!" Annie said cheerfully. "I'd like to introduce my parents, John, and Mary. Mom, Dad, this is Lizzie, and her husband Donny."

"Nice to meet you both," Mary responded with a warm, inviting smile. "We've heard so much about you! Nice to finally put faces to names. Please, join us."

"Thanks," Donny replied as he pulled Lizzie's chair out for her, then took his seat beside her.

"I understand you live in Tulsa," Lizzie mentioned. "What brings you to North Texas?"

"The book fair," Mary beamed. "My favorite author on the planet has a meet-and-greet scheduled this afternoon, and John surprised me with tickets!"

"That's so sweet," Lizzie exclaimed. "I bet you're excited."

"I am," Mary confirmed. "Would you two like to come with us? It starts at two-fifteen."

"Thanks for the invite, but after we eat, we're heading to the mall," Lizzie revealed. "I'm not usually big on shopping, but I'm in the very rare mood to get some done. We don't have anything at all for the baby yet and I just feel like we shouldn't wait on it any longer."

Their waitress appeared at that moment and Donny and Lizzie placed their food order.

"A Monte Cristo? You sure?" Donny asked, and Lizzie nodded vigorously.

"It's what sounded good – and you and I both know it's not the strangest thing I could have ordered."

Mary chuckled.

"This one," she began, thumbing Annie's direction, "had me craving fish pretty much the entire nine months. I wasn't much of a seafood person before I got pregnant, and I haven't touched it since."

"I do love seafood," Annie joined in with a wicked grin. "Sorry, mom."

The five continued to make small talk, pausing briefly when the first round of food arrived, and again when Lizzie's and Donny's sandwiches were brought to the table.

Chapter Sixteen

It wasn't long after lunch, the monkeys, and the meerkats that Charlie was worn out. He fell asleep with his head on Nathan's shoulder as he was carried out to the car.

"I'm surprised he lasted as long as he did," Bella murmured as they walked.

"I am too, actually," Nathan agreed, fishing in his right front pocket for the keys to remote-start their SUV. "I'm also thinking he's got the right idea. A midday nap wouldn't kill any of us."

"How long has it been since we had the chance to take a nap together?" she asked as Nathan opened the back door and maneuvered a still sleeping Charlie into his car seat.

"I honestly can't recall. If I had to guess, I'd say that the last time was way before our son was walking and talking."

"So, we're way overdue," she said with a wink and a smile. "That's my take on it."

Within twenty minutes they were home. Nathan gently picked up their sleeping child, carried him inside, and put him to bed.

Then he followed Bella down the hallway to the master bedroom. He paused long enough to check his cell phone.

No new messages or emails. That's unusual – and a good sign, I guess?

He turned his cell phone's volume down to 'vibrate only' mode and set it on his bedside table, then removed his shoes and socks and stretched out beside his wife.

"This is weird in the middle of the day," Nathan whispered, and she giggled.

"Shush, I'm trying to take my nap."

At long last, John glanced at his watch, then signaled for the check.

"It's a quarter to one," he said. "And I know you wanted to check out some of the vendor tables before the meet-and-greet, honey."

"You're right, I did," Mary confirmed. "I guess we'd better get going, then."

Once Annie's father settled the entire bill – Donny protested but was politely overruled - the five stood and made their way out to the sidewalk, where Mary stepped forward and hugged Lizzie and Donny both.

"It was great to meet you both, and hopefully we'll get a chance to spend time together again someday," she said earnestly, and made Lizzie smile.

"I'd really like that. Annie can keep you posted on whatever baby shower dates come up, and you're welcome to come and celebrate with us."

"Delightful! Yes, count me in. Annie, you'll let me know, right?"

"Of course I will! Okay, you two have fun shopping - and I'll see you tomorrow, Lizzie.".

Donny and Lizzie watched the trio cross the street to head toward the convention center a few blocks down.

"Annie and her folks are nice people," he declared.

"Very nice," she agreed, then sighed happily.

"Ready for the next round of walking?"

"Yep. Let's get out of this heat and into the mall."

Donny shook his head.

"So weird to hear you of all people say that."

"Tell me about it."

The moment they got past the automated doors at the convention center, Annie Adams could sense her mother's excitement kick into overdrive, and it brought a grin to her face.

And she had to admit, she was excited too; what they'd walked into was an absolute reader's paradise.

Books were literally *everywhere* they looked. Colorful displays drew the eye to tales of dragons and magic, of suspenseful mysteries, of undiscovered galaxies, of 'happy-ever-after'.

Behind them she heard her father chuckle softly to himself. He knew, as did she, that she and her mother were both completely captivated by their surroundings.

"It's huge," Mary marveled, her eyes wide, swiveling her head from left to right. "Where on earth should we start?"

"Well, I see a pretty interesting looking setup right over there," John pointed out. "And I know how you love a good cozy mystery, honey. How about we start with that one?"

As Mary cheerfully headed toward the display he'd indicated, John lingered back with Annie long enough to whisper, "I think I'm going to need to build her some more bookshelves."

"I believe you're right," Annie said with a laugh. "I see a display off to the left I want to check out. Do we want to reconvene back here in a half hour, or should I just find you guys at the meet-and-greet?"

Her father handed her a meet-and-greet VIP ticket.

"I have no idea how caught up your mother might get," he said, "so, you'd better plan on meeting us in there."

"Fair enough."

"What about this one?" Lizzie asked an hour later, holding up a onesie with *Little Angel* stenciled on the front.

"I like it! Grab a few in different colors."

"Speaking of colors," she said as she picked up three more and draped them over her arm, "do you want to know ahead of time if we're having a boy or a girl?"

"My take on it is, I really don't care, so long as the baby is healthy," Donny responded immediately. "So, the question is, do *you* want to find out ahead of time?"

"I think I do, yeah."

"Then that's what we'll do. Hey, how about these?" he said as he pointed out a pair of the tiniest sneakers either of them had ever seen.

"I think he or she will be a ways off from those," Lizzie replied. "But they can go on the 'for future reference' list."

"That's becoming quite a list. Did you have any idea about all this stuff?" he asked as he waved his arm around the store. "Because I have no clue what half this stuff even *is*, much less what it does, Liz."

She raised her right eyebrow.

"How the hell would I know, either? I mean, the only kid I've ever spent any time around is Charlie, and I didn't even know him until he was already a couple of years old. Completely missed the first part."

She turned to him and took his hand.

"So, I guess we'll just have to figure it all out together as we go along."

The space designated for the closeout session of the book fair was a long, rectangular room with polished cherry-wood flooring. At the far end, a dais had been placed, complete with podium and microphone setup.

Directly behind that, the fair's organizers had meticulously staged a heavy, thick two-piece black curtain, then adorned it with a full-size banner and silver metallic streamers that cascaded from the banner's corners all the way to the floor.

Hank Myers and Gabe Crosson stood side-by-side behind the curtain, counting down the final minutes until her name was announced to what was turning out to be a rather full house.

"I'm going to step out into the audience now," he informed her. "And don't worry. I'll keep watch, all right?"

"Okay," Gabe replied, her voice as smooth as ever, a subtle twisting of each ring on her right hand the only sign that the stress of the whole ordeal was beginning to get to her.

"We'll catch them, Gabe, I promise you," he murmured in her ear. "You go out there and be brilliant. The team and I have this covered."

She squeezed his hand and took a deep breath, then squared her shoulders.

"I've got this," she said confidently. "I'll see you after."

He nodded and smiled at her reassuringly before he turned and made his way past the stage-right edge of the curtain.

<hr>

Unbeknownst to Hank, while he was attempting to calm Gabe's nerves, Annie and her parents took their seats in the audience.

Annie had ducked out of the main exhibit area at one-fifty-five to make sure that her mom and dad had seats up close to the stage. She'd managed to snag three together at the end of the fifth row and had guarded them as she texted her dad to let him know where to look for her once they entered the room.

John and Mary joined her at ten minutes past two.

"Look what I found!" Annie's mom whispered to her as she dug four glossy hardcover books out of the new plastic bag she carried.

"Nice!" Annie whispered back. "And I bet you get through all of them in a single weekend."

Her dad nodded his agreement, then looked around the room.

"Great seats, Annie-bug. Nice work."

———

Hank leaned against the wall on the left side of the room, his focus on the makeshift stage, and applauded along with everyone else when the session's moderator introduced Gabe.

Another book fair worker standing nearby closed the distance.

"Hey! How's it going?"

"Not bad," Hank murmured. "Last event."

"I know, right? I'm glad they opted to put fewer chairs in here for this one," Hank's uninvited confidant told him. "Last session in this room, there was only enough room to walk single file between the front row and the dais."

"That does seem a little crowded," Hank observed, mentally noting the roughly fifteen feet of space from the dais' edge to the first ten-seat row of folding chairs.

"Tell me about it," the other man quipped under his breath. "At least someone came to their senses and put some space between this time. And man, I'm glad they fixed the microphone! Can you imagine if she had to try to talk to all these people without one? Thank God that tech guy saved the day."

"What tech guy?" Hank asked, a small fist of alarm blossoming in his gut.

"The tech guy," the worker repeated. "He was in here like, I don't know, thirty, forty minutes ago, maybe? Changed out the whole setup."

Hank's pulse quickened as his focus narrowed to the podium

where Gabe stood and was just beginning to speak. At first, nothing looked out of place, a normal podium with an everyday all-purpose microphone.

And then he saw it.

A subtle red blink, blink, blink from somewhere underneath the podium's solid oak top that reflected against the metallic streamers behind and on either side of Gabe.

He instinctively raced forward.

From her seat on the right end of the fifth row, Annie was startled to see a sudden blur of motion ahead and left of her position.

In the split second she caught a glimpse of the man's face and realized it was Hank, she knew something was very wrong. Without even thinking twice about it, she yanked her badge and weapon from her purse, clipped them both to her belt, and rose to her feet.

Annie stepped into the aisle, hands raised, and began to shout, even as she watched Hank leap onto the dais and bodily tackle Gabe Crosson in a single smooth motion.

Hank and the author landed hard amidst shocked gasps from the audience, then rolled, dropped off the back of the dais, and disappeared underneath the bottom of the curtain.

"Get down! Get down! *Everybody down! Now!*" Annie screamed as she ran forward to close the distance to the spot she'd last seen Hank.

She had just managed to get alongside the first row of chairs before time seemed to stop altogether, and for a precious second, Annie could hear nothing at all. She felt heavy, like she was bogged down, sprinting into a fierce headwind, swimming in molasses.

As a result, it was more surprising than painful when she was suddenly and violently picked up and flung backward and to the right like a rag doll, a bright red-orange ball of flame racing forward with a deafening roar to meet her.

That can't be good, was Annie's last conscious thought before she came to rest on the cherry-wood floor almost twenty feet away.

———

Behind the curtain, Hank shook his head to clear the cobwebs brought on by the blast, then looked over at Gabe.

Thank God for that stupidly thick curtain, was his first thought. *This could have been so much worse...*

"What... the... *hell?*" a wide-eyed Gabe managed, still trying to catch her breath; Hank's tackle had knocked the wind out of her.

"Are you okay?" he asked, and she nodded.

"Just... winded...," she wheezed.

He glanced up to see Marlon and Sam, two of his team members, crouched down next to them.

"Find the guy that was standing beside me," Hank told them. "Skinny kid, eighteen, maybe nineteen, five foot nine, brown hair, goatee, and glasses. He's wearing a dark blue polo shirt and khakis. Find him and hold him. He got a look at whoever rigged the podium to blow."

"On it," Marlon assured him.

"And get Gabe checked out with a medic, then take her back to HQ," Hank directed Sam, who nodded.

"Gabe, I need you to go with Sam now. I need to try to find whoever messed with the podium. Okay?"

She nodded, tears brimming.

"Thank... you...," she whispered.

"Thank me later, once I've nailed this guy," he answered, and squeezed her hand before he got to his feet.

He walked around the left edge of the curtain and froze at the sight that greeted him.

Chaos. Pure chaos.

In addition to setting off the room's automatic sprinkler system, the detonation had sent chunks of solid oak podium in all directions –

particularly, the middle four seats of the first two rows. Hank saw at least three session patrons that were obviously dead, and he startled as both sets of double doors in the right-hand side wall were flung open and the facility's emergency services team converged on the scene.

He stepped forward, skirting the edge of the ruined dais, his eyes tracking back and forth across the carnage-filled room to try to figure out where he could help the most.

A loud shout from the far right side of the room drew Hank's attention, and the realization of what he was seeing almost dropped him to his knees.

It was a battered, bloodied, and unresponsive Annie, and the young man in the medic uniform trying desperately to revive her held the portable defibrillator's paddles against her chest and shouted "Clear!" again just as Hank reached her side.

Chapter Seventeen

It was two-thirty when Donny and Lizzie opted to take the ice cream break they'd talked about.

"Let's go to Braum's," Lizzie prompted. "They have the best sundaes."

"Braum's it is," Donny confirmed, and they strolled out of the mall and to his truck, placing the four shopping bags of baby paraphernalia they'd acquired in the back seat.

Lizzie had just clicked her seatbelt into place when Donny's cell phone made a peculiar noise.

"What on earth is that?"

"I signed up for breaking news alerts," he replied as he punched in his code to unlock his phone and scrolled to the notification.

He scanned it, then whipped his head to the right to look at Lizzie.

"What?"

"There's been some sort of explosion... at the convention center."

Lizzie paled.

"Oh, my God... Annie and her parents!"

She pulled out her own phone, dialed Annie's number, and waited.

After five rings the call connected.

"Annie! We just heard! You guys okay?"

"Lizzie?" a deep male voice answered.

Lizzie infused her scowl into her voice when she grumbled, "Who the hell is this?"

"It's Hank. She's hurt, Liz. She's... really hurt."

In the background noise beyond Hank's voice, Lizzie could make out the word "clear" and then a sound that made her blood run cold – a defibrillator humming, then firing.

"*Jesus*! What happened?"

"I can't talk now, Liz. They're loading her for transport to Harris and I need to drive her parents over there."

"We will meet you there," Lizzie babbled. "I'll call Nathan, and we all will meet you there."

She hung up the phone and turned to look at Donny with tears already beginning to overflow.

"Harris," she rasped against a sob. "We need to head to Harris Hospital."

"What happened?"

She relayed Hank's side of the conversation as Donny raced them toward Fort Worth's hospital district. When she was done, Lizzie called Nathan's cell phone several times.

She got more and more frustrated with each attempt.

"Drop me off, and go find him," she pleaded as Donny pulled into the emergency room parking lot. "Nathan will never forgive himself if he's not here and she...".

He reached over and wrapped his arms around her.

"We can't think like that," he urged. "We *have* to keep the faith and believe she'll be okay. And yes, I will go find him and bring him here. All right?"

"Okay," Lizzie managed.

"Go, honey. I'll be back as soon as I can."

She flung open the truck's door, leapt out, closed it, then ran like hell toward the emergency room entrance, dialing the Director's number as she went.

Donny barely let his truck touch the pavement in Nathan Thomas' driveway before he braked hard, slammed the transmission into park, and jumped out.

He sprinted to the front porch, rang the doorbell twice, then began to knock.

"What the *hell*?" he finally heard Nathan snarl.

"Thank God you're home. We need to go," Donny shouted just as Nathan opened the door, hair tousled, feet bare, and service weapon in hand.

"Dude. You scared the hell out of us. Why are you banging on my door?"

"Why didn't you answer your phone? There's been an explosion. Annie's been hurt. We need to go. *Now*."

"Give me ninety seconds," Nathan assured him, and sprinted back down the hallway to his bedroom to put his socks and shoes back on.

A groggy Bella was standing beside his nightstand, holding his phone in her hand.

"You missed five calls from Lizzie," she said, and yawned as she held it out to him. "And two from the Director...What's going on? And who was pounding on our front door?"

"Donny's here. Some sort of explosion and Annie's injured. I don't know more. I have to go," he explained in a rapid-fire staccato as he finished tying his shoes, then took his phone back, kissed her cheek, and raced out of sight.

He shoved his handgun and phone into their respective holsters and clipped them to his belt on his way back to the still open front door where Donny was waiting.

"Read me in," a solemn Nathan instructed as they climbed into Donny's truck.

"Right now, there's not much more to tell. Some sort of explosion at the convention center around two-twenty this afternoon. Annie and her parents were there attending the book fair, and from the sounds of things, they were in the vicinity of where the explosion happened. Hank said that she was badly hurt and was being loaded up and taken to Harris Hospital. That's all I know. Lizzie couldn't reach you, so she asked me to find you when I dropped her off in front of the emergency room."

Donny glanced over at him when they stopped at the red light.

"You might want to call Liz back, Nathan. She didn't say it, but when you didn't answer I think she was worried something had happened to you, too."

"I was asleep," Nathan muttered, his voice full of self-recrimination and regret. "I hadn't had a single email or call today, and all three of us were tired from hiking around the zoo, so I decided to join Bella and Charlie for a nap. *That's* why I missed her calls. I turned my ringer down so I could take a freaking nap."

"Hey, hey, easy now," Donny reassured him. "Dude. You had no way of knowing any of this was gonna happen, and you're not a robot. You're allowed to stop and catch your breath occasionally."

"Not when I am responsible for a team whose jobs can get them killed, I'm not," Nathan growled. "And you can sure as hell bet that I won't make that mistake ever again."

He dialed, waited, then pulled the phone away from his ear when Lizzie's voice blared, "Oh, my God! Are you okay? *Where the hell have you been?*"

"I'm fine, Liz, and I'm sorry I didn't answer earlier. I'm on my way to Harris with Donny right now. What's the status?"

"They finally got her pulse back in the ambulance, but Hank said they had to shock her several times," came the reply. "Last we heard, she's stable for now, but she's intubated and still unconscious."

"We're about ten minutes out," Nathan replied. "Has the Director been notified?

"Yes, and he's on his way."

"Thanks. Meet you in the ER."

"You got it."

Lizzie and Hank were standing side-by-side and speaking with the Director when Donny and Nathan walked through the double doors of the emergency room. The Director saw them and waved them over.

"My guy's pulling video feed from the venue," Hank said without preamble as he reached out to shake Donny and Nathan's hands. "We should be able to view what happened from several angles within the hour. We also have an eyewitness that saw the guy that did this, and we've got him talking to a sketch artist."

Nathan nodded.

"I'll call Rick and get him up here. We'll need his eyes on the video, too," he replied, then glanced around the crowded waiting room.

"Is there somewhere else we can talk?"

The Director pivoted to speak to one of the nurses at the triage intake desk, who pointed to her left.

"This way," the Director intoned, and the group followed him to a smaller waiting room about seventy feet down the hall.

Once they'd all settled in, Nathan leaned forward.

"What the hell happened today?"

Hank scrubbed his hands over his face.

"The intended target was Gabe Crosson," he revealed. "She's had a stalker after her for a while, and she feared something like this happening, so, she hired us to protect her."

"Who's *us?*" the Director asked.

"Cosantóirí," Hank replied. "Private security firm. And yes, we'll gladly work together with the FBI to catch this guy."

"Noted. Proceed."

"Anyway, we've kept a close eye on her all week long. We figured he'd go for the big splash, and we were right, but we weren't able to stop it from happening."

Hank sighed.

"He rigged the podium to explode. I happened to be standing next to our eyewitness at first and he mentioned the microphone swap-out. Then I saw a red blinking light reflecting in the streamers. I ran up and grabbed Gabe and got her off there and we tumbled off the back of the platform. Next thing I know, *boom.*"

"Is she okay?" Lizzie asked.

"Bumps and bruises, and it scared the hell out of her, but otherwise she's fine," Hank confirmed. "We got behind that great big heavy curtain just in time, and the device was a good five, five-and-a-half feet off the floor, so, we were below the main blast trajectories."

He looked around at the group.

"We were lucky. Really lucky."

"What about everybody in the audience?" Donny asked.

"I didn't look around long once I saw Annie on the floor," Hank confessed. "But from the glimpses I got, there were severe injuries and some fatalities in the first two rows at least. Her mom got a nasty cut on her arm, and her dad has a small contusion on his left temple. They rode here with me, and they're being checked out right now."

"Where were Annie and her parents seated?" Nathan interrupted.

"I don't know, and I didn't think to ask. I didn't see them in the crowd. My focus was on Gabe, especially once I saw that blinking light."

He sighed again and pulled out his cell phone.

"I'll see if Marlon or Sam knows. Marlon was directly across the room from me, and Sam was more toward the back."

Within ten minutes, the group had some answers.

"Annie and her mom and dad were sitting at the very end of the fifth row," Hank divulged. "Marlon and Sam both told me that when I started running toward Gabe, Annie immediately left her seat and started running forward and shouting at everyone to take cover. Marlon said she was parallel with his position when the blast happened. Which means she was roughly twenty feet from it."

He swallowed hard.

"Marlon *also* said her actions saved lives. Some people listened to her, and because they did, their injuries were far less severe than they could have been. Sam said the same thing."

Lizzie noticed that at this news, the Director pulled out his notepad and pen, wrote several sentences, and put the items back in his pocket.

A knock on the doorframe had the entire group turning their heads to check out the newcomer. It was a woman in scrubs and a long white lab coat.

"For Annie Adams?" she asked, and receiving unified nods as confirmation, she stepped into the room and shut the door.

"I'm Dr. Miller, head of cardiothoracic surgery. Annie's been stabilized and is doing well."

"Surgery?" Lizzie asked. "She's going to need surgery?"

"Not necessarily, ma'am," Miller replied. "I was brought in as a consult to run further tests and make sure that what happened to her today didn't cause permanent damage to her heart."

"And?"

"So far all tests have been clear," the doctor confirmed. "We believe at this point that Annie suffered a very rare phenomenon called commotio cordis. Basically, a blow to the chest wall, even a very slight blow, can send the heart into arrythmia if the projectile hits the chest with just the right speed, angle, and timing. A few milliseconds sooner or later in the heartbeat cycle, and commotio cordis doesn't happen. We most often see it in sports like baseball and hockey, so, most cases on record involve young athletes."

"What's the prognosis?" Hank asked.

"Typically, it's not great, because no one on scene realizes what's happening, so the patient doesn't get the right treatment soon enough. But in Annie's case, starting CPR and using a defibrillator happened right away. She should make a full recovery."

Hank groaned with relief as he leaned forward and cupped his head in his hands.

"Matter of fact," Dr. Miller continued, "We've already been able to extubate her. She's on pain medication for the time being because aside from the commotio cordis, her body took a beating from the concussive forces of the blast. It also ruptured her right eardrum, and it will take a couple of weeks for her hearing to return on that side."

"I know firsthand how all that feels," Lizzie reminded everyone. "She'll be sore for *at least* a week."

"We're FBI agents," Nathan chimed in. "Would she be cleared for field duty?"

"Eventually, yes, barring any complications, she should be able to resume her normal activities," Miller replied. "But keep in mind that while Annie is quite healthy, this event caused her to *literally* have a heart attack. So, post-cardiac arrest protocols are in place here, which means we will be moving her to the cardiac care unit, where she will remain for the next couple of days."

The Director stood to shake Dr. Miller's hand.

"Thanks, doc. Any chance we can see her?"

"Her parents are in with her right now, but yes. One at a time, five minutes at a time. You can rotate through."

"How are they?" Hank asked.

"Both had very minor injuries," came the answer. "A cut, a contusion, and a pair of mild concussions, from what I understand."

"We'll need to take John and Mary to our house," Lizzie immediately said to Donny. "They'll want to stay in town until Annie's out of the hospital, at least, and they should be around people who know what to watch for if they both have concussions. Plus, they've already met us, so, they'll be more comfortable staying at our house rather than in some random hotel."

"Absolutely. We'll make that happen," he confirmed.

As they all followed Dr. Miller back into the hallway, both Hank's and Nathan's phones began to ring. Hank moved a few feet away to answer his; Nathan maintained his position right next to the Director.

"Thomas," Nathan answered, then listened, and after a few moments said, "We'll be right there."

He disconnected the call and looked at his boss.

"That was Dr. Adamal, sir. He wants to see us. Diane Mackinaw's awake."

"We should head up to the fourth floor, then, and we can see Annie when we're done up there," the Director answered as Hank strolled back over to rejoin the group.

"According to Marlon," Hank announced, "the convention center videos are ready. We can review them at Cosantóirí. It's not far from here."

Nathan turned and looked at Lizzie.

"Can you reach out to Rick for me?"

"Happy to. What am I telling him?"

"To meet us over there in about an hour."

With that, Nathan and the Director headed toward the elevator.

"I'd like to go see Annie now, please," Hank said quietly, and Dr. Miller nodded.

"Sure. Right this way."

Chapter Eighteen

A STOIC HANK stood beside Dr. Miller and patiently waited his turn as her parents each kissed Annie's cheek, then stepped out of her triage room.

"Oh, honey," Mary Adams cooed when she saw him, and immediately grabbed him and enveloped him in a hug. "There, there. She's gonna be just fine, young man, don't you worry."

He gratefully returned the hug, his ability to speak temporarily paralyzed by the surge of emotions that suddenly overwhelmed him.

Hank felt a calloused hand land on his shoulder, and he raised his tear-stained face to meet John Adams' gaze.

"I think my Annie-bug's sweet on you, you know. You might ought to do something about it once she gets out of here."

"I plan to," Hank managed. "Because I love her, sir."

"Good to hear, son. And I know you're both grown and you don't need it, but just in case you're wondering, you have my blessing," the man replied, then gently nudged his wife and said to her, "Let him go, honey, so he can go in and see his sweetheart."

Mary released him and stepped back, and Hank took a moment to wipe his eyes with his sleeve, then cleared his throat.

"Remember, stay on her left side so she can hear you," the doctor reminded him, and Hank nodded.

"I'll be back in a few minutes," he told them, then turned and walked into Annie's room.

He took a deep breath and just gazed at her for a long moment. Her brown hair was striking against her pale, bruised skin. She'd suffered cuts to her arm, torso, and face; her right cheek had been bandaged.

He exhaled slowly before he strode over to the left side of her bed.

"Hey, you," he said, his voice quavering as he reached out to take her left hand in his.

Her eyes opened, blinked twice, and slowly shifted in his direction.

"Hi," she managed. "You okay?"

He leaned in close to make sure she could hear what his heart had to say to hers.

"I'm fine, other than you scared the hell out of me. Don't ever do it again. You hear me? Never again, Annie."

She frowned behind the oxygen mask and shot him a look that clearly screamed *risk comes with the job, duh.*

"Agent," she rasped, and closed her eyes again.

He grinned for just a moment at her stubbornness.

"I... okay, fine, I get that. And you're not just an agent, you're a badass agent, and we both know that won't change. So how about this instead. Please don't run into danger *without protective gear* ever again. Okay? Promise?"

She answered, "Promise," in a whisper.

"Good. Because *I love you*, understand? I love you, and I need you, and I didn't realize how much until I saw you lying there on that floor. I thought you'd left me, and it damn near broke me."

Her eyes popped open again, searching his.

"Love me?"

He nodded, fresh tears surfacing.

"With all my heart, Annie."

She squeezed his hand, smiled, and murmured, "Love you too," before she drifted back into a healing sleep.

———

Three floors above, Diane Mackinaw was not only awake, she'd come up swinging, and Dr. Adamal met them at the elevator to give them the latest update on her condition.

"The short version from a neurological standpoint is, she will most likely need to walk with a cane from now on. I'd say she got lucky; the permanent damage could have been much, much worse," he told Nathan and the Director.

"When did she wake up?"

"About forty minutes ago. She came to and started to pull out her breathing tube. Fortunately, someone was in the room taking her vitals when she awoke. I've done a preliminary neuro check, and other than some weakness on the right side, she's doing well. Our ear, nose and throat specialist is on his way to examine her larynx. He should be coming by in the next half-hour, and he'll be able to better determine if she suffered permanent damage to her vocal cords."

"Thanks, Dr. Adamal," Nathan said, and shook his hand before he and the Director walked down the hall and into room 4003.

———

The moment she saw Nathan come into her room Diane demanded, "Sketch artist" in a gravelly voice.

"Easy, Diane. Easy," he soothed as he sat on the side of her bed. "Take it easy. Don't overexert yourself."

The Director stepped to the foot of the bed.

"I take it from your statement just now that you remember what landed you in the hospital."

Diane nodded, her green eyes blazing with fury.

"Get someone to draw," she grated, then swallowed and grimaced. "Catch bastard."

Nathan grinned as he patted her hand.

"Let me talk to your doctors right quick, and make sure you're cleared to do some talking, okay?"

She nodded again, a little calmer.

"I'll be right back."

He stepped out into the hall and headed for the nurse's station.

"Hey there. Diane Mackinaw in room 4003," he said. "She's awake and alert and is requesting we get a sketch artist in here so we can draw a composite of what her attacker looked like. I know she has a throat injury. Should she be talking much right now?"

"It's best for her if she switches to pen and paper, at least until after the specialist comes by to examine her," the lead charge nurse on duty told him. "I can bring some in."

"That's what I thought. Yes, she'll need a pad and pen please."

"Someone will bring it shortly."

"Thank you."

He turned on his heel and went back into Diane's room.

"You still need to limit your talking," he told her. "But we're going to get you a pad and a pen, and get our guy up here to draw for you, all right?"

Diane gave him two thumbs up then opened her arms wide as Mia came flying into her room.

"You're awake! Thank God!" her daughter exclaimed, then burst into tears as she hugged her. "I was so worried, Mom."

"We'll give you guys some privacy," the Director suggested, and motioned toward the door.

Once he and Nathan were in the hall, the Director announced, "I'll stay with Diane and arrange for the sketch artist. You go check on Annie, and then get yourself over to Cosantóirí and watch those videos."

"Yes, sir," Nathan answered, and moved with purpose toward the elevator to go see for himself that Annie was truly going to be okay.

By the time Nathan returned to the triage unit, it was his turn to step in and check on her. He didn't stay long, sensing immediately that undisturbed rest was what Annie needed most, and after patting her hand he rejoined the group in the hallway.

"We're going to move her to the cardiac care unit on the fifth floor," Dr. Miller announced. "I mention it again because there are much stricter visiting hours up there. I don't know that we'll be able to get her settled in before visiting hours stop at five o'clock."

She turned, studying John and Mary's expressions.

"And the two of you look exhausted," Annie's doctor said gently. "Between being injured yourselves and worrying about your daughter, I'm sure you are worn out."

Annie's parents shared a silent exchange.

"I think probably the best thing we can do is let Annie sleep and go back to the hotel and try to get some sleep ourselves, John," Mary said plaintively.

Lizzie stepped forward.

"Actually, Donny and I would love for the two of you to come stay with us," she offered. "We think you'll be much more comfortable at our house, and you're welcome to stay as long as you need to."

Annie's parents exchanged another long look before John answered.

"We accept your invitation," he said. "Thanks. It means a lot."

"No problem at all. We're happy to have you," Donny answered. "So, let's go get your things from the hotel, and Lizzie or I can drive your truck to the house, too, if that's all right."

"That's fine, thanks."

"Great! We probably ought to get going, then," Lizzie chimed in, and turned to Nathan.

"Let me help get them settled, and then I can meet you over at Hank's office."

"Works for me," Nathan replied, and shifted his attention to Hank.

"You ready?"

"Sure. Need a ride?"

Rick Conner was already standing in the lobby of Cosantóirí chatting with its CEO Allen Jones when Nathan and Hank arrived.

"How's Annie?" was his first question to them.

"She's gonna be okay, thank God," a visibly relieved Hank answered. "But whoever planted that device killed some people and seriously injured a bunch more. And he may or may not know yet that he didn't succeed in achieving his primary goal – hurting or killing Gabe Crosson. The sooner we catch him, the better."

"Which is why I've got the videos queued up and ready," a solemn Marlon called out to them from the hallway leading to the conference room. "Right this way, gentlemen."

"I'm surprised the Director's not here," Rick remarked as they walked.

"Diane woke up and she's insisting on giving a statement and working with a sketch artist," Nathan informed him. "The Director opted to take point on that piece."

"Fair enough. Glad she's awake – and from the sounds of it, none the worse for wear, I assume?"

Nathan's jaw set.

"They don't know how much permanent damage she suffered yet. Adamal seems to think she won't be able to walk unaided, and the throat specialist hadn't been by yet before I had to leave."

Rick pursed his lips as he mulled over the information.

"Well, we'll just have to hope for the best. It's a miracle she survived to begin with."

Lizzie unlocked the front door, then held it open for John and Mary as they climbed the front porch steps. Donny trailed behind them with their suitcases in hand.

"The guest room is right this way," she prompted once they were all inside and she'd shut the door.

"You have a beautiful home," Mary mentioned as they walked through the living room and down the hall.

"Thanks! Lot of renovations after the blast. This house was originally built in the 1970's, so, we took the unexpected opportunity to update some things when we rebuilt it."

Mary turned to her, confused.

"Blast? What blast?"

Lizzie smiled.

"I guess Annie never mentioned it? And it's kind of a long story, so, how about we get your suitcases squared away, then make some tea and visit?"

Now it was Mary's turn to smile.

"That sounds delightful."

In short order, the Adams' belongings were tucked safely into the guest room bureau, and the four of them headed into the kitchen.

"I don't know about the rest of you, but I'm starving," Lizzie announced. "Lunch feels like it was forever ago."

Donny took point and told their guests, "I'm happy to whip something up for us."

"Something simple like sandwiches is fine," John assured them. "You've already helped us out by letting us stay here."

"Or pizza," Mary added. "And we're buying, and we won't take no for an answer."

A grinning Donny replied, "Fine by us. We never say no to pizza around here. Just tell me what you like on yours, and I'll get them ordered for us."

Once the food order was taken care of, Mary took a seat at the table and leaned forward, resting her arms on the wood surface.

"Now, tell me about that blast. What on earth happened?"

"The short version is, someone had a grudge against a co-worker of mine named Jones, and my house became ground zero," Lizzie began as she added water to the teakettle.

Mary's eyes sparkled with curiosity as John's eyebrows shot skyward.

"Well now we just *have* to hear the long version."

———

Allen took point in making introductions between his staff and the visitors, then said, "Please be seated. Marlon, whenever you're ready."

Marlon dimmed the overhead lights and the first video recovered began to play on a huge drop-down screen at one end of the conference room.

"This is the footage from inside the session room," he explained.

They all watched silently. Hank's tension level was almost palpable when the video showed a tall, muscular man with a badge clipped to his shirt and carrying some sort of satchel approach the podium and begin removing the original microphone.

"Hold," Nathan requested, and Marlon dutifully hit 'pause'.

"Rick, you see this?"

"I do," Rick confirmed.

"See what?" Hank asked.

"That microphone setup. It's wireless. If it were a legit exchange, they'd have just swapped out end pieces," Rick explained. "Which confirms for me personally that this guy was up to something."

Play resumed, and sure enough, they witnessed Gabe's stalker remove a corded microphone from his bag, complete with a small, rectangular mass through which the cord threaded.

"Hold again, please."

This time the request came from Hank's teammate Sam, who lumbered his six-foot-seven frame forward toward the screen.

"Can you zoom in?"

Marlon did just that.

"Yeah. I'd bet my life that's got C-4 in it. See that right there?" Sam asked the group as he touched the screen itself to indicate a small area on the rectangular object. "There's your light. It's just not armed yet."

"Thanks, Sam. Let's keep going," Allen directed.

Hank's eyewitness came into view, and Hank watched the young man as he placed copies of the session's program in each empty chair, then looked over the entire setup before he nodded his hello to the man at the podium and left the room.

The mystery man finished setting his lethal trap, then gathered up his bag and left the room quickly.

"Okay," Hank said. "So, by around one-fifty this guy was done and out of there. Let's watch the rest of this one, and then I want to see *exactly* where he went after he left this session room."

Marlon nodded.

"Already have them lined up for us."

"Oh, my," Mary Adams exclaimed when Lizzie reached the end of her tale. "So, is the cartel still after Jones? What happened to him?"

"Shortly after all that, the cartel ran into money issues, it seems," Donny answered. "They kind of... imploded is a good word for it, I guess. Jones got word that things had improved, so, he came out of hiding. Matter of fact, the kid just landed a job not far from here."

The front doorbell pealing caused Donny to rise to his feet.

"Dinner's here. Be right back."

Back at Harris Hospital, Diane, the Director, and a very talented sketch artist had made huge strides.

Dead grey eyes, she wrote on her pad and showed them. *No emotion, no soul in them at all. Just... flat. Like a snake's eyes.*

The artist nodded and altered his sketch accordingly, then turned it around and showed it to her.

She began to tremble so badly that she couldn't keep a firm grasp on the pen.

"That's him," Diane rasped, wide-eyed and terrified. *"That's him."*

The video resumed play over at Cosantóirí, and they all saw Annie come into camera view and lay claim to three seats at the end of the fifth row.

Hank chuckled despite the severity of the situation as he watched her repeatedly wave off others' attempts to occupy the chairs she'd picked.

"What's so funny?" Nathan murmured.

"I remember noticing the room was *packed* when I left Gabe's side and went around the curtain," Hank replied. "No wonder Annie was guarding those seats like they were made of gold."

The group fell silent again until the moment Hank sprang into action onscreen and rushed to the stage.

"Hold, please," Allen said, then looked over at Hank. "Do me a favor and fill us in on what was happening at that point."

Hank relayed having the conversation with another event worker, then seeing the light reflected in the streamers.

Allen stood and moved to look more closely at the screen for a moment, then nodded and pointed.

"Yep, right there."

He strode back to his seat.

"If you hadn't mentioned it, I wouldn't have even noticed it."

"If that kid hadn't said something about the microphone being replaced, I might not have either," Hank admitted with a frown. "All the threatening letters Gabe had received had me thinking that whoever was after her was an amateur. A psycho, but an amateur. But *that* guy? That guy's had at least *some* training in handling explosives."

"Absolutely," Rick chimed in. "Because he knew *exactly* how much to use to confine the blast to one room and not take out the whole building. Wouldn't you agree, Sam?"

Everyone looked across the room at the resident explosives expert, who folded his massive arms across his chest and corroborated Rick's statements with a single solemn nod.

With the press of a button, the footage continued.

Chapter Nineteen

Hank's attention immediately shifted over to Annie rising from her seat and running forward, waving her arms frantically, her long brown hair flowing behind her.

The sight of her stole his breath, and his hands clenched into tight fists as he witnessed the way she was bodily thrown first backward, then downward when the podium disintegrated into flames and chaos.

Beside him, Nathan reached out and laid a hand on his shoulder in silent support, both riveted to the events playing out on the massive wall monitor.

"Hold, please," Hank said gruffly, and Marlon obliged.

"She saved people," Rick commented into the silence. "I noticed at least twelve people in the first four rows ducked down. If they hadn't, they'd likely be dead. I assume she was shouting warnings as she ran forward?"

"Yes, she was," Marlon confirmed. "And seeing this playback confirmed another thing. Annie got *very* lucky. If she'd been any closer, well...".

Nathan's phone ringing pierced the sudden, weighty lapse in

conversation.

"Sorry, one moment," he said as he stood and squeezed Hank's shoulder, then stepped out into the hallway.

"Thomas."

"Nathan," the Director intoned, "Diane gave us one hell of a composite. I'm on my way to you now. I'd like to see those convention center videos myself."

"Yes, sir, absolutely. We've just finished the first one, but I'll have them set something up where you can view it before we move forward as a unit on the others."

"Thanks. See you shortly."

Nathan retook his seat and announced, "My director is on his way to view the security footage."

He glanced over at Rick, and continued, "And I think we just caught a huge break. It sounds like Diane really came through on providing a suspect description for our current cases."

"Speaking of description," Hank said to Marlon, "Let's rewind and see if we can get any clear close-up still shots of *our* suspect, for comparison with our eyewitness account."

By the time the Director arrived, Marlon had not only captured three usable still shots from the first round of footage, but he'd set up a laptop and headphones so the Director could review the first session, then arranged the second video to appear on the big screen.

"How about we take a coffee break while he gets caught up?" Hank murmured to Nathan as the Director was introduced to everyone, then guided over to the listening station.

"Yeah. I could use some caffeine myself," Nathan agreed.

"Follow me. The breakroom's right this way."

They walked side-by-side down the hallway.

"I already knew what happened, and it was *still* hard as hell to watch that just now," Hank managed as he grabbed two mugs from the cupboard, filled them both, and handed one to Nathan. "She just looked so... so....".

"Small and helpless?" Nathan offered as he accepted the beverage, and Hank closed his eyes and exhaled with a heavy sigh.

"Something like that, yeah."

"Well, we both know firsthand that Annie Adams is much, *much* tougher than she looks," Nathan reminded him, and Hank chuckled.

"She is. It's part of why I love her," Hank responded earnestly, then glanced over at a pleasantly surprised Nathan, who'd located the creamer and sugar stash and was stirring some of each into his coffee.

"You love Annie? Hank! That's awesome," Nathan exclaimed, his smile genuine.

"I think so, too. And you want to know a secret?"

"Lay it on me."

"She's the only woman I've ever said that to who wasn't a family member."

Nathan nodded his understanding.

"Been there, with Bella. That's a big deal."

"A *really* big deal."

"Okay, and? What happened? Did she say it back?"

"Well, yes, she did, but she's *also* doped up on pain medications at the moment, so," Hank faltered. "I guess we'll need to revisit the subject once she's clear-headed, just so there's no misunderstandings."

"Sounds like," Nathan agreed. "And just go forward from there. But my gut says her answer won't change."

He leaned over and clapped Hank's shoulder.

"I'm happy for you, man, I really am."

At that moment Rick appeared in the doorway.

"Nathan, Hank, you guys really need to come see this," he intoned, his face serious but his eyes dancing with excitement.

When they returned to the conference room Nathan and Hank noticed that a composite sketch had been pinned up on the board on the far left-hand side of the room. Next to it was a crisp, clear, close-up picture of the man responsible for the explosion at the convention center.

"*Wow,*" Nathan muttered as they strolled over to view them more closely. "This sketch is amazing! It almost looks like a carbon copy of the still shot. Hank's eyewitness even noticed the small scar transversing the right eyebrow."

"It's uncanny," the Director agreed as he moved to join them, then paused.

"And it's even more significant than you think."

"How so?" Hank asked.

"Because that is the sketch based on *Diane Mackinaw's* description, not the kid from the book fair."

Nathan's and Hank's jaws dropped wide open.

"So. This guy's responsible for four separate murders that we know of, plus the people he killed in the bombing," Nathan snarled. "We have a final tally on that yet?"

"Before I left the hospital, I was able to confirm that five people died instantly, and at least fifty more were injured, twelve of them critically. The death toll could increase," the Director confirmed, then turned to his counterpart, the head of Cosantóirí LLC.

"Mr. Jones," the Director began, "I believe now is an excellent time to extend our working relationship even further."

"I concur," the man replied. "And please, call me Allen. I had a feeling that this might run late, so, dinner should be here any minute. I hope everyone's okay with sandwiches. We can eat while we watch the other security videos. After that, I suggest bringing my guys up to speed regarding your other cases. Manpower, surveillance tools, whatever you need. All our resources are now officially at the FBI's disposal. We will help in any way we can."

"Much appreciated, Allen."

"Before we start the videos, I'd like to reach out to the lab and get any results they have so far on that second bottle of red clover supplements," Nathan interjected. "That will help determine some of our next steps."

The Director signaled his acknowledgement, and Nathan stepped back out into the hallway. Before he called his lead lab tech, he fired off two quick texts.

The first was to Lizzie, asking her to join them.

The second was to Bella to let her know that he wasn't sure when he'd be coming home.

Fifteen miles away from Cosantóirí LLC, Lizzie plucked her phone from her belt holster and skimmed Nathan's message.

"Duty calls," she announced, and rose from her usual spot on the couch. "You good?"

"We're fine, Liz. Go," Donny urged her. "See you when you get back."

She leaned over and kissed him before grabbing her service weapon, wallet, and keys and heading out to her car.

Donny grinned over at John as the front door closed.

"You like baseball? Because there are three different games on right now."

"I'm a fan, but she's not," John said with a wink as he tilted his head to indicate Mary.

"That's my cue," she quipped with a smile. "I'd like to go lie down for a while anyway – or at the very least, read."

Within the half-hour both dinner and Lizzie had arrived, and the group gathered once more around the long, narrow conference table.

Hank made short work of introducing Lizzie to his boss and co-workers, then asked, "We ready to get started?"

Hearing no dissenting opinions, Allen gestured to Marlon, who announced, "Okay. The one we're about to review is from the camera in the west hallway, right outside the session room. I picked this one to watch next based on the suspect's direction of travel after he planted the device."

He clicked 'play' and all attention turned to the screen on the south wall.

As they watched, Lizzie murmured, "So you already checked out the footage from *inside* the session?"

"Yes," Nathan murmured back, and pointed past her to the laptop open on the credenza. "It's queued up ready to go over there, if you'd like to see it when we're done with these others."

"Noted."

The man they sought came into the camera's view at one-fifty-one, and the entire team was shocked to see him casually stroll over to occupy a cushioned two-seater bench directly opposite the session room's doors. The suspect unclipped the badge from his shirt and shoved it into his satchel, then pulled out a book and began to read.

"Why just sit there? What is he *doing*?" Lizzie asked aloud.

"Blending in – and killing time," Sam answered. "Most likely the explosive he's planted has a very short transmitter range. That would make the most sense. And we should be able to prove that out here shortly."

Rick glanced down at the notes he'd taken during the initial video viewing.

"Detonation in the first video occurred at two-twenty-one," he reminded the group. "Let's just keep watching. If Sam's right about the range, we should see this guy pull out his phone a few minutes before then."

***

Annie blinked several times, then frowned in confusion. She turned her head to the left to see a woman in scrubs standing by the bed.

"Where," she started to say, then coughed a little.

"You're awake! Glad to see it. My name's Danielle, and I'm on shift tonight as your nurse," the woman explained with a warm smile. "I was just checking your vitals. They're all good. You're doing well."

"Where am I?"

"Cardiac care unit," Danielle revealed. "The blast stopped your heart, and we got it going again. So, you're in here with us for the next day or two as a precaution, just to make sure there's no permanent damage."

Annie swallowed, then grimaced.

"Water?"

"Sure. I bet your throat's a little sore from being intubated."

Danielle deftly picked up the plastic cup with the bendy straw and held it for Annie to drink.

She did so, gratefully.

"Thanks. My whole body hurts."

"I can imagine," her nurse sympathized. "It's my understanding that you were thrown about twenty feet, Annie. You want some more pain meds?"

"No, thanks, not yet. I don't like the brain fog they bring with them. Where are my parents?"

"I'm pretty sure they would have left to go get some rest when you were moved up here, since visiting hours for this unit end at five o'clock, and you got up here a little before six. But they'll be back tomorrow morning."

"Are they okay?"

"I honestly don't know," Danielle told her. "I came on shift at six. But I can find out and let you know, all right?"

Annie nodded, then closed her eyes as Danielle made a few quick notes in her chart and left the room.

She dozed for a few minutes, until a recent memory shot to the forefront of her mind and rattled her back to being fully awake – and grinning from ear to ear, despite her entire body feeling like she'd been run over by a large truck.

Hank said he loves me.

As the timestamp reached two-eighteen in the video, the suspect put away his book, then stood, slung his satchel across his body, pulled out a cell phone and rapidly pressed a few keys. He paused a moment, smirked, and began to walk nonchalantly down the hallway to the main foyer, where he turned left.

He walked out of the west hallway's camera range at two-twenty.

"Find him, Marlon," Allen urged. "We need to trace his escape route."

"Yes, sir."

"And if we can catch him, we'll be able to run diagnostics on his phone and *prove* he set the thing off," Rick finished, earning a grin from Marlon even as the Cosantóirí tech's focus remained on getting the right video footage up onscreen next.

"There's one thing I just don't get," Nathan pondered aloud, and brought all activity in the room to a standstill.

"What?" Hank asked him.

"This guy's been careful. I mean, *really* careful," Nathan explained. "Up until the bombing, he's taken great pains to conceal who he is. He hacked and deactivated security systems. No fingerprints at any of the four murder scenes. Diane had physical trace under her nails from fighting back, but if our guy's DNA isn't on file anywhere that won't help us find him. Up until today, he's been smart."

Nathan stood and walked to the board containing the still photograph.

"And then he does *this?* He knowingly puts himself on camera in a very public and highly populated space? No gloves? No attempt to hide his face? Something just isn't right here."

The rest of the group was stunned into silence at first by

Nathan's observations – until Rick rose and closed the distance to where Marlon's laptop was in action.

"May I?" he asked, and Marlon vacated his chair with a grin.

"By all means."

Rick sat down and rapidly typed a series of commands, then turned his attention to the big screen.

"Okay, see this?" he asked the small crowd as he stood, walked over, and pointed at long lines of coded gibberish displayed for all to see.

"I see it, but I don't get it," Nathan replied. "What the hell is all that?"

"I do! I see it!" Marlon enthused as he rushed to join Rick.

"Right here! See that? Our guy *did* try to disable the security cameras," Marlon explained. "And he did succeed – on the primary ones. But the convention center has *two* sets. Complete redundancy, totally different servers, and the backup set isn't connected to the rest of the network. You can tell which set of security videos you're looking at by the numbers embedded right *here*."

Rick grinned and said, "Man, it's nice to have someone else around who speaks my language."

Then he turned his attention back to Nathan.

"What all this means is that he's good enough to hack a system, but not good enough to even consider that what he's hacking just might have fail-safes in place. He's self-taught on the electronics piece, for sure. Anyone properly trained in subversive electronics knows to think *at least* five steps ahead and account for contingencies."

"Or he *did* search, but because the backup set is a standalone and not wired into the internet, he didn't see it," Marlon quipped behind him.

"So, he only *thinks* he got in and out without being seen," Nathan muttered. "Boy is he gonna be surprised when these videos are submitted into evidence at his trial."

"But every bit of this brings up other major questions that we still haven't answered yet," Lizzie interjected. "Besides their killer, what the hell do a retired schoolteacher, a financial planner, an FBI secretary, and a pediatric dental assistant have in common? And how the hell would *any* of them tie into a bombing?"

"On the surface, they don't," Nathan answered. "Which is why first thing tomorrow, we're going to keep digging."

He turned to Allen Jones.

"Can we borrow Hank?"

"Sure. You want to set up shop here, or at your place?"

"Over in Dallas," Nathan answered. "Among other things, our lab's only two floors away if we need information or test results."

"Very well," Allen agreed, then looked over at his men.

"Until further notice, you're assigned to the FBI, Hank. Transfer any active cases to other team members."

"Like old times," Hank said with a grin. "What time tomorrow, Nathan?"

"Eight-thirty all right? That will give us time to collate all the data - and I also figured you might want to swing by the hospital to see Annie first."

"You're right, I do. Thanks."

"I'll keep looking at these videos," Marlon offered. "By the time you guys get together tomorrow morning, I'll be able to tell you *exactly* where and how our bomber left the premises."

Rick said, "So, Marlon. Fellow Navy, am I right?"

"Got it in one," came the reply. "Retired at the twenty-year mark."

"Excellent! If you have a few minutes, I have a couple of ideas I want to bounce off you," Nathan heard Rick say as he and Lizzie moved toward the door.

"Rick won't be leaving anytime soon, you know that, right? He's found a kindred spirit," Lizzie murmured, and made Nathan grin.

Chapter Twenty

By six-thirty a.m. Monday morning the Thomas household was lively. Nathan had taken point on feeding and dressing Charlie so that Bella could get ready for her first day at her new job.

"I can drop Charlie off at daycare, if you guys need me to," Sarah offered to Nathan as she sipped her hot tea. "Or he can stay home with me today. I'm happy to watch him. Whatever you want to do."

"I've got it, but thanks. I appreciate the offer," her brother replied with a smile. "Besides, aren't you supposed to go sign stuff and pick up keys today?"

"I *wish* it was moving that fast," Sarah said on a long exhale. "The waiting's been driving me *nuts*, even though I only put the offer in two days ago."

Nathan chuckled at her.

"You have to give it time, sis," he admonished, and she rolled her eyes.

"Please dear God, don't say it..."

"You know," he continued, a mischievous smirk on his face, "there's a poem that will...".

"*Noooo*," Sarah said loudly, and laughed. "I do *not* want to hear Mom's infamous patience poem again, please and thank you."

He shrugged, his eyes sparkling with mirth.

"Suit yourself."

Nathan turned his attention to Charlie.

"Hey, buddy. Let's go kiss Mommy goodbye before we get going," he suggested, and watched Charlie run down the hallway at top speed.

Nathan opted for a more leisurely pace, reaching the master bedroom just in time to hear Bella say, "Thanks, sweetie. Have a great day today. Love you!"

"You sure you don't want to just drive over with me?" he asked again.

"I'm not ready yet, and I don't want to hold you up," she answered with a rueful smile.

"All right. Do you want to have lunch together today?" he asked her as he enveloped her in an embrace.

"I'd like that," she replied as she turned her face upward for a kiss. "How about I text you?"

"Works for me," he said with a grin, then looked down at Charlie.

"You ready, buddy?"

"Yep. Bye, Mommy!"

And with that, the energetic four-year-old led the charge back down the hallway.

"I love you. See you at lunch," Nathan murmured, and kissed her again before he too headed toward the front door.

Hank rapped lightly on the overly wide doorframe of room five-oh-five a little past seven a.m., and Annie's eyes lit up.

"Hi," she said softly as she watched him approach and pull a chair up close to the left side of her bed.

"Hi," he said with a smile as he took her hand. "How are you feeling?"

"Ugh," Annie responded with a grimace. "Did you know it's damn near impossible to sleep in a hospital? Just as I drift off they come back in to poke and prod me and take my vitals. I don't think I slept for more than fifteen minutes at a time last night. And I ache all over. I think being run over by bulls in Spain would've sucked less. I'd rate my experience with explosive devices as zero out of ten. Do *not* recommend."

He chuckled at that and reached up with his other hand to gently stroke her hair.

"I bet."

Her eyes met and held his.

"So about yesterday," she began.

"I won't hold anything you said against you," he told her. "You were doped up."

"Oh, no you don't," she retorted. "You told me you loved me. No takebacks."

Hank's grin morphed into a megawatt smile.

"You remember that, huh."

"Yeah, I remember that. I also seem to recall telling you I loved you too."

"Like I said, they had you on some pretty powerful stuff," he replied, "so you weren't responsible."

Annie's left eyebrow arched.

"You think I was so drugged up that I would just say that to someone and not mean it?"

He shrugged, then yelped when she reared back and punched him in the shoulder as hard as she could, given that she was cooped up in a hospital bed.

"*Ow*," Hank muttered, and frowned at her. "Fine. You meant it."

"I really did," she said softly, and watched his smile come back in spades.

"You did?"

"Yeah."

The hand that had been stroking her hair moved to cup her cheek lightly as he stood, leaned over the bedrail, and kissed her.

When they came up for air, she murmured, "Now get me out of here. I can be sore and achy just fine at home."

Hank shook his head at her.

"I'll be surprised if they let you out today, honey," he told her earnestly. "You do realize that you were thrown about twenty feet, right? Not just a straight line, either. *Up*, and back. And your heart *stopped*, Annie. I watched them zap you more than once to get it going again. If all that doesn't call for staying your sweet ass right here in this bed and taking some time to heal, I don't know what does."

He had to bite back a smirk when she began to pout.

"Fine," she finally snarled. "But can you at least, I don't know – bring me my laptop or something? I really need to keep working the case I'm on."

"Um, hello? Twenty-foot toss followed by a heart attack? I think Nathan will be just fine with you resting for now. We've got this."

"We?"

"I got temporarily reassigned to work with Nathan," he explained. "Our mystery bomber and your mystery killer are the same guy, it seems. Diane Mackinaw's eyewitness sketch mirrored a still shot from the convention center footage. I'm headed over to Dallas to meet up with Nathan when I leave here."

"Seriously? Oh, man. Now I really need you to bring me my laptop! I can even make do with paper copies of the file. *Please?*" she pleaded.

"Nope, not gonna happen unless the doctor clears it. And you're in the cardiac wing, so, I doubt that it's gonna be a yes on that one," he answered. "So, you're going to have to wait until you get home."

"*Dammit,*" Annie muttered under her breath. "You are so mean sometimes. But you know I still love you, right?"

"I do," he said with a twinkle in his ice-blue eyes. "We've established that. But please continue to tell me all you want. I love hearing it."

"Good. Then you know that I'm saying this with all the love in my heart. I'm telling you – get me outta here, bring me something to work on, or leave, Hank."

His eyebrows raised.

"My God, you're stubborn. That is so... *sexy*," he murmured as he leaned down again to kiss her cheek.

"Love you. I'll see you this afternoon, baby."

He stood, winked, and walked out, Annie rolling her eyes behind his back as her fierce scowl morphed into a slight smile.

***

By seven-twenty-five, Bella was one hundred percent convinced she was going to be tardy on her very first day.

Dammit. I should have just caught a ride in with Nathan. Not the best way to start my career here, she grumbled under her breath as she continued her search. The morning's influx of people traveling to their downtown jobs had made it crystal clear - her prior ability to find a parking spot within six blocks of her destination had most likely been a fluke.

Fifteen minutes elapsed before she finally found a vacant space twelve and a half blocks from her building. She pulled in, shoved the transmission into park, and heaved a huge sigh of relief.

Maybe once I get my feet under me I can ask about the possibility of working remotely one or two days a week, she told herself as she quickly gathered her things, exited the car, and made sure it was locked before she began her long trek to work.

***

Hank Myers arrived at the FBI's Dallas office building at eight-seventeen. He wound his way through the lobby's security checkpoint and met Nathan at the first-floor elevators.

"Morning," he grinned as Nathan pressed the call button. "I'll assume that coffee's a foregone conclusion. Haven't had any yet."

"Absolutely."

When they got to the eighth floor, they headed straight for the conference room to find Lizzie and Rick arranging thick stacks of paper at four place settings.

"Come on in, gonna be a long day," Lizzie told them. "I made copies of each case file to review, including crime scene photos, any lab results, and any victim histories compiled so far."

"After we get some coffee, that is," Nathan interjected. "First things first, Liz."

Lizzie's narrowed eyes made him wince.

"*Fine*," she ground out. "I'll just go ahead and get started listing the salient points on the board while you go get your precious coffee."

"What was that about?" Hank asked as he and Nathan made their way to the breakroom.

"Coffee. She's mad that she can't have any."

"What Neanderthal doctor told her that?"

"A doctor didn't. The baby did," Nathan shared as he poured himself a cup. "Every time she's tried to have some it's made her sick."

"Oh, man, that's gotta suck."

"I wholeheartedly agree. I hope for her sake that it doesn't last much longer. Usually, she drinks even more of it than I do."

Nathan added cream and sugar to his mug, then stirred, sipped, and sighed in contentment before he asked, "How's Annie doing?"

"Beat up and hurting, so, she's grouchy," Hank replied as he took his turn at the coffeepot. "And stubbornly insisting on going home already, but you and I both know she'll be in there another day, at least. When she heard I was officially working with you guys on all this, she asked if I could bring her laptop to her, or at least a case file to look at while she's in there."

Hank held up a hand before Nathan could speak.

"And I already told Annie I wasn't going to do either one. I told her that once she's home, it might be a different story, but that for now, she needs to rest and heal."

"And what did she say to that?"

Hank's face broke into a wide grin.

"She said she still loves me even though I'm mean - and then she threw me out of her room."

Nathan laughed out loud as he checked his watch, then gestured toward the door.

"Come on, let's get back in there so we can get started."

Once they had returned to the conference room, Nathan picked up the narrative thread.

"Lizzie asked two excellent questions last night – what do our murder victims have in common, and how would any of them link to a bombing?" he began, then extended his right arm out in a sweeping gesture.

"I believe the answers lie somewhere in these pages. Hank, I need you to sub in for Annie on a couple of things. First, you're on point to drill down into Sybil Planchett's background. I know Annie had been looking into it already, so, at least some results should be here in the case file copies. Pick up where she left off. Second, you'll need to go down to the lab on six and get a copy of any test results on that second bottle."

"You got it," the ex-DEA man answered, and stood. "I'll get the lab run done now so that we have the data."

"Good! That gives me time to add some more bullet points," Lizzie announced as she retook her position in front of the ample rectangular whiteboard hung on the east wall.

As Hank left the room and Lizzie added facts about each victim, one of Rick's laptops at the end of the table began to chime.

Rick stood and quickly closed the distance to scan his results, then grinned at Nathan.

"I *knew* it," he announced. "Guy's using a combo. I thought he might be, but my analysis just proved it."

"A combo?"

"Remember how I said that his IP was tracing back to a coffeemaker?"

"Yes. And?"

"That's called piggybacking. But that's not the only layer in place. The short, non-tech version is, he's using more than one approach to help conceal his location," Rick said. "But I started running a facial recognition program this morning, using the picture that Marlon emailed over. Between that and my being right about how the guy performed his hacks, I should have him run to ground for you soon."

"How soon?"

"Sometime tomorrow at the latest."

Then Rick stood upright, folded his arms across his chest, and waited for the inevitable question.

As was his habit, Nathan started to ask his brother-in-law if he was sure but stopped himself just in time, a move that was both noticed and very much appreciated by Rick.

"Oh, my poor baby," was the first thing Mary Adams said when she and John entered Annie's fifth floor room in the cardiac unit. She immediately went over and tried her best to envelop Annie in a gentle hug, given that the bedrail was blocking full access to her only child.

"I look worse than I feel, Mom," Annie reassured her as she

returned the embrace, knowing full well that it was, at the very least, a little white lie.

Because I feel like hell... Maybe it's a good thing I don't have my laptop with me. I'm too tired to do anything...

"How about you guys? Are you all right?"

Mary turned her loose, stepped back, and held up her left forearm so that Annie could see the bandage wrapped around it.

"I got a cut and your dad got a bump on the head. Other than that, we're fine, honey."

"Thank God."

Her father John strode to her bedside to take her hand.

"How much longer do you have to stay in here, Annie-bug?"

"Doctor Miller came by about ten minutes ago and said that if things stay like they are, they'll move me to a regular room this afternoon. After that, I might get to go home Thursday."

Sarah answered her cell phone on the third ring.

"Hello? Yes, this is Sarah Thomas. Yes. Yes, ma'am, absolutely. Wednesday at ten a.m. is perfect. Yes, I'll see you then. Thanks so much."

She disconnected the call, then squealed with excitement. The perfect space she'd found to fulfill her dreams would be officially hers before the week was out.

With a mile-wide smile, Sarah sat down in front of her laptop, flipped her notebook back to the page labeled 'kitchen equipment', and began to verify pricing for the things she was going to need.

"Lab results," Hank said, and held up some papers as he walked back into the conference room and took his seat.

"And?" Nathan asked.

"The short version is, both bottles had all the same stuff – one hundred percent foxglove."

Lizzie dutifully updated the corresponding bullet point listed under Sybil Planchett's name before she and Rick rejoined them at the table.

"So, where should we begin?" Rick asked.

"Demetrious Winger," Nathan suggested, "since Lizzie already has a lot of data on him. After that, we need to take some time and dig into the other victims' backgrounds like we'd already planned. Then we'll reconvene this afternoon at four and go over everything in more detail."

He glanced over at Lizzie and said, "Walk us through Winger's case, please."

Chapter Twenty-One

"DEMETRIOUS WINGER," Lizzie began as she stood and moved back over to the board on the wall.

"Caucasian male, forty-six, six feet one inch tall and one hundred ninety-five pounds, according to the autopsy report. Black hair, brown eyes, goatee. No tattoos or other readily identifiable marks. Official cause of death was exsanguination due to a severed carotid. He was divorced and lived alone in Grapevine. No children. Closest living relative is his older sister who resides in Las Vegas."

Lizzie paused to take a small sip of water.

"He was a certified financial planner and stockbroker who worked from home. He'd been self-employed the last two years; prior to that he worked for a couple of very well-established brokerage houses for thirteen years."

"Pretty standard, then," Hank mused.

"Very vanilla," she confirmed. "No criminal record at all, not even a parking ticket. The worst things I've uncovered so far have been a few fines from the public library. Social media accounts were all benign as well."

"Drilling down into his financials, his expenses align with his income, no dramatic swings or mysterious gaps. If he *did* have any secret accounts at all, financial or otherwise, I couldn't find them," she added, looking over at Rick. "Maybe you'd have better luck with that part?"

"I can try," he agreed. "I'll adjust my parameters on the diagnostic of his computer to try to ferret them out as well if they exist."

"I also waded through his accounting records and customer lists. No one stood out. His invoicing seemed to be in order, no exorbitant charges that I noticed. But I'm not very well versed at all when it comes to stocks and trading and accounting stuff, so, there could be something that I've missed," Lizzie finished.

"Let's tag in home office on that piece," Nathan suggested. "Get Maria Morano involved to cross-check Winger's business records for any anomalies."

"Sure. I'll reach out to her when we're done here," Lizzie confirmed.

Hank looked up from his copy of the Winger file that he'd been skimming to follow along while Lizzie talked.

"Says here his murder was actually caught on video?"

"Yep," she replied. "I believe Rick has it queued up, if you'd like to see it."

At Hank's nod, Lizzie moved to pull down the projector screen along the far wall, while Rick pressed a button on the laptop directly in front of him, then got up and turned off the overhead light.

They watched the entire video that tech support employee Steph Bronski had been quick-thinking enough to record.

Hank winced and muttered "*sweet Jesus*" at around the three-minute mark, to which Nathan said quietly, "Yeah, we all felt the same way when we watched it for the first time, too."

Once the video ended, Rick flipped on the lights again.

"Speaking of... *that*," Nathan said and gestured at the now-blank screen, "did you get a chance to run calculations to try and get a lead on our killer's height?"

"Not yet," Lizzie replied. "That was next on my to-do list from

Saturday afternoon. But now we have the convention center video footage to work with too, and using those would be *much* faster."

"Absolutely," Rick answered immediately. "Marlon already sent copies over to us. Before I continue with my individual research into Sugar Phillips, I can set that up as well. It should be able to calculate the suspect's height for us in a matter of seconds."

He looked across the table at Nathan.

"Marlon also said to tell you that the bomber left the premises via a service entrance in the southwest corner of the building."

"Any external cameras?"

"Yes, and Marlon's already trying to retrieve that footage for us, as well."

"Thanks. Lizzie, anything else?"

"My next steps are to cross-reference the other victims' names in relation to Winger," she revealed. "I want to see if his life intersects with any of them at all."

"Very well. Hank, we can set you up in the bullpen," Nathan advised him.

"Give me just a few minutes to get his user access restored," Rick advised. "I want to make sure he doesn't have any login issues."

Rick moved again to one of his laptops to type in the height calculation commands, then to another to reactivate the user profile that Hank Myers had used during previous visits.

"There, all done," he told them, and handed Hank a sticky note with his temporary password. "And our killer is six feet, two and a half inches tall, by the way."

"Thanks, Rick," Nathan said. "Okay, guys, let's get moving. We'll meet back in here at four p.m. sharp."

With that, they dispersed. Hank walked with Lizzie and Rick back out to the bullpen area, while Nathan retreated down the short hallway to his office and closed the door, mentally steeling himself for the unpleasant task of invading a co-worker and friend's privacy in his search for answers.

Three blocks away, Bella Thomas had waded through all her onboarding paperwork with the office manager by nine o'clock.

"Okay, that should be it, then," the woman said with a smile. "Let me show you to your office!"

They walked side-by-side down the hallway, and along the way her guide pointed out to Bella where the breakroom, office supply closet, and restrooms were located.

Roughly three-quarters of the way down, the office manager stopped at a door on the left.

"Here you are," she announced, and waved Bella through and into the office space. "I'll leave you to get settled in. If you need anything, just come see me."

"Thanks, Valerie."

Bella opened the credenza's bottom drawer and set her purse inside before she turned on her computer, glanced at the slip of paper with her username and password, and attempted to log in.

User not found.

Bella double-checked that she didn't have her caps lock key turned on or her numbers lock turned off, then tried again, only to get the same result.

"O...*kay*," she murmured to herself, then stood and made her way back to the manager's office.

"Hi. My login information doesn't seem to be working," she told Valerie, who frowned at that bit of news.

"Hang tight," the woman answered, and dialed a three-digit extension.

"Hey there. Bella Thomas. Did you complete her setup?"

She listened, her frown deepening, as Bella watched from the doorway.

"Yes, *please* get that done right away. Thanks," she said abruptly, hung up the phone, and looked at Bella.

"Sorry about this. Not sure which part of *this is urgent* wasn't clear to him earlier."

Bella smiled.

"No worries, it happens. I'll just give it a few minutes, then try again."

She retreated to her office, and just to be on the safe side, she waited ten minutes before she tried to log in again – and sighed deeply at the result.

User not found.

Bella dissipated some of her frustration by mentally uttering a couple of swear words in each of the four languages she spoke before she tried to login a third time.

Welcome! the display read at last, and her next sigh was one of relief.

The corners of her mouth turned upward into a smile when she opened her company email for the first time and noticed that right after the obligatory 'welcome aboard' message, her new boss had sent her three others, all with project documents attached.

Bella made sure that she fired off a 'successful login' confirmation to Valerie first, then opened inbound message number one to finally start her workday.

It was close to noon before Lizzie knocked on Nathan's door.

"Come in," he directed, and she entered the room.

"How's your search going?"

"Fine, I suppose, for snooping through a colleague's personal life," he grumbled, his distaste for the task evident in both his voice and expression. "And, just like Winger for you, exactly zero has turned up so far that is useful in any way. There's a strong possibility that none of the victims knew each other at all."

Lizzie shrugged as she sat in his visitor's chair.

"You know, we could save ourselves some time and just ask Diane directly if she knows any of the others," she prompted. "And we can ask Sybil Planchett's daughter too, I suppose. But I don't know if Winger's sister would be much help on that front, and I have no earthly idea about Sugar Phillips' next of kin."

Nathan's cell phone chirping disrupted the conversation.

"Sorry, hang on a sec, Liz," he said, then pulled his phone from his belt holster and read the text.

"It's Bella," he shared. "She's ready for lunch and she's about to walk over here. Would you like to come along, help celebrate her first day of work?"

"Sure," Lizzie replied. "I'll go grab the guys."

We'll meet you out front, Nathan texted his wife, then saved his work and locked down his computer.

Perfect timing, he thought to himself. *Prying into Diane's life this way is giving me a headache. Good to walk away from it for a bit. Besides, maybe when I come back to it something will stand out that can help us catch this guy...*

Bella's smile was brilliant as she closed the distance to the quartet loitering in front of the drab gray ten-story building.

"Hi!" she said to them all as Nathan leaned in and kissed her cheek.

"How's the first day going so far?" Lizzie asked as they began to walk briskly toward Nana's Café.

"Well, once I was finally able to log in, it improved a great deal," Bella said wryly. "But I *still* can't access anything on the network but my email. So, my boss told me to take an extended lunch to give the IT guy time to get it all corrected. First day snafus. Part of it, I guess. How're things up on eight? Making any headway?"

"It's painstaking," was all Nathan would say.

Bella winced.

"That bad, huh?"

"Not *bad,* per se," Rick chimed in. "Just... time consuming. But hopefully, we'll catch a break before today's out."

In no time at all they were being led to their usual spot by Sherrie, who took their orders, then hustled back with drinks and rolls.

"I'd like to propose a toast," Hank said as he held his glass of iced tea aloft. "To Bella and her new job. May they get the tech bugs worked out quickly."

"Thanks, Hank," she replied as they all clinked glasses. "Hey, you should join us on Memorial Day! We're having a get-together at the house. Burgers and hot dogs."

"I'll try," he told her. "But to be honest, it's largely going to depend on what's going on with Annie at that point. If she's feeling up to it, we'll be there."

"Fair enough. How's she doing?"

"Not happy being stuck in the hospital, for starters."

"I can imagine," Bella answered solemnly. "Every time I've been cooped up in one sucked....".

Her head tilted to the side as she thought about it.

"I take that back. The day we had Charlie. That was the only good visit – if a hospital stay can ever be considered 'good'. But the other two times? *Nope.*"

"I'm pretty sure it's not on *anybody's* 'favorite things list'," Hank rejoined with a laugh, and was met with murmurs of agreement all around the table.

"Well, I hope she gets to go home soon," Bella told him.

"Me and you both."

***

A few cities over, the subject of their conversation was currently out of bed without supervision. John and Mary Adams had left to go have lunch.

Annie, bound and determined that she didn't need to call a nurse just to use the bathroom, had stubbornly launched herself off the bed and into a standing position. Gripping her IV pole tightly in her left hand and trying to hold her gown closed in the back with her right, she took two steps forward.

Unbeknownst to her, her balance was severely skewed, thanks to both her concussion and her ruptured eardrum, and she shrieked loudly as suddenly her entire world tilted hard to the right.

"Whoa! What are you doing?" a booming voice behind her said as massive arms kept her from falling to the floor.

Annie looked up and over her shoulder to find a huge man staring down at her with a frown.

"S-s-sorry," she stammered self-consciously. "I just needed to use the bathroom."

He pulled her upright enough to sit her down on the side of the bed.

"Stay there. I will get you a nurse," he instructed, then reached over, pressed the call button, and explained what was needed.

The stranger waited with her until her assigned nurse arrived.

"Thanks, Toby, I've got it," the nurse said, and the stranger nodded once, then left.

"Who was that?" Annie asked.

"Toby's one of our respiratory techs," came the reply. "And it sounds like you're lucky he walked by when he did. Otherwise, you could have had a nasty fall."

"I guess I'm more banged up than I thought," Annie admitted.

"Ya think?" the nurse said with a grin.

A sheepish Annie Adams allowed herself to be helped first to the toilet and then back into bed.

Nathan glanced at his watch right after he handed Sherrie his credit card to pay for the meals.

"It's ten past one," he told Bella. "What time do you have to be back?"

"By one-thirty," she answered. "So, we could stroll leisurely, and I'd *still* get back with time to spare."

Rick's cell phone chimed repeatedly, and he glanced at his screen, then over at his brother and sister-in-law.

"Or maybe, just a little bit quicker than leisurely?" he suggested. "Because according to this alert, my program just pinned down his true location. I think we got him, Nathan."

"Yep, we need to get moving, then," Nathan confirmed as he accepted his card back from Sherrie.

"Sorry, honey," he told Bella, who waved him off.

"It's fine, really. And now, I'm kind of glad I drove myself in – because it sounds like you might be late getting home tonight."

The team wasted no time getting back to the eighth-floor conference room, where Rick made a beeline for his bank of laptops.

"It's a location out in Lake Worth," Rick shared as he confirmed the street address, then began to cross-check Tarrant County Appraisal District records to pin down the property owner.

"Betty Mirelander," he announced to the group. "Let me see what I can find out about her."

After a few minutes of serious keyboard time, he began to grumble under his breath.

"What?" Nathan asked.

"She's dead, according to this obituary from six weeks ago," Rick growled.

"Okay, so, not her. But someone with access to her property, maybe?" Lizzie said. "Next of kin?"

"Or another piggyback scenario. There are no living relatives listed at all," Rick replied with a heavy exhale. "And even if she *was* still alive, she couldn't have been our killer anyway. Not in the Winger case, at any rate. The photo in the obituary listing proves it. She was only sixty-three, but wheelchair bound."

Rick scoped out the progress on another laptop.

"No results with facial recognition," he reported, his shoulders slumped to match his frustrated tone. "This guy's not popping up at all, not even with the Texas Department of Motor Vehicles. *Dammit.*"

After a few moments' silence, Nathan cleared his throat and told the group, "Those are setbacks. They are not the end. Rick, keep that IP trace program running; maybe it will ping to a different location. Expand the facial recognition search nationwide. We'll each continue building our victim histories, including cross-checking whether any of them intersect with each other *or* Betty Mirelander, and reconvene at four as originally planned."

Four o'clock arrived faster than Hank expected, and he found himself sinking into a conference room chair with nothing extraordinary to report concerning one Sybil Rios Planchett. Just like Demetrious Winger, nothing stood out, and she seemingly had no connections to her fellow victims.

But he took center stage when prompted and walked the group through the main points of his research, as Lizzie had done before him.

"Sybil Rios Planchett, Hispanic female, aged sixty-seven. Per the autopsy report she was five feet eight inches tall and one hundred sixty pounds, with gray hair and brown eyes. Cause of death was digitalis poisoning which led to cardiac arrest, as confirmed by lab testing done on both her and some supplements found in her Benbrook home. She has one adult child, a female, who lives across town from her. Her husband preceded her in death seven years ago."

"Ms. Planchett was a retired schoolteacher; she spent forty years teaching sixth grade English. Nothing amiss was found in her financials and cross-checking her against the three other victims and against Betty Mirelander returned no results."

Next it was Rick's turn. And once again, not only was Sugar Philips pretty much a model citizen, but he *also* could find zero points of intersection with the other three victims.

"Sugar Philips, a twenty-five-year-old African American female, five feet nine inches tall and one hundred sixty-five pounds. Official cause of death was insulin overdose, brought about by what was first thought to be a defective pump. Lab testing has since proved that the pump was operating as designed and that its programming was intentionally altered. Ms. Philips lived and worked in Mansfield. She'd been a dental hygienist for a pediatric dental practice for the past few years. She was single, with no relatives close by; she originally hailed from Memphis, Tennessee and from what I found, her family are all still there. No criminal record at all, and her expenses aligned with her income. I found no evidence that she was connected in any way with any of our other victims or with Betty Mirelander."

Chapter Twenty-Two

NATHAN FINISHED the round by sharing data about Diane Mackinaw. Nothing remarkable surfaced in his search through her life, and just like the others, no obvious commonality to the other three had been found.

"Diane Mackinaw, Caucasian female, aged forty-seven, five feet five inches tall and one hundred thirty-seven pounds. She's been employed with the FBI for almost twenty years now. She's divorced and lives alone in Keller; her daughter Mia, nineteen, attends college up in Denton, Texas at Texas Woman's University. Diane's ex-husband moved to the East Coast twelve years ago and per my research has not come back to this area in the last four years. She was attacked in her home and manually strangled but survived, and her overall prognosis is good. Her financials are pristine, and there's no evidence that any other individual in these cases, including Ms. Mirelander, intersected her life at all."

Then he returned to his seat and slammed his hand on the table in frustration.

"But there *has* to be something," Nathan stressed. "Something, however small, that ties them all together. Something that caused them all to land on this whack job's radar in the first place. What are we not seeing?"

He leaned back in his chair, his elbows on the armrests, his fingers steepled together under his chin, and closed his eyes.

"Gabe Crosson. *Gabe Crosson*," he muttered after a long silence. "Hank, you said Crosson was the intended target at the convention center."

"Yes, she was."

Nathan's eyes flew open.

"Lizzie – you said Winger had records of paid library fines in his checking account, right?"

"Yes, he did," Lizzie confirmed.

Nathan looked at Hank and Rick.

"What about Sugar and Sybil? Did they have anything at all in their profiles relating to books?"

Both men shuffled back through their recent case file notes.

"Sugar Philips had a Tarrant County library card," Rick offered.

"Holy crap. So did Sybil Planchett," Hank breathed.

Nathan pulled out his phone, dialed, and waited.

"Hey, Mia, it's Nathan Thomas. Are you with your mom right now? Okay, great. Can you ask her if she has a Tarrant County library card? She does? Thanks, Mia. Please tell her I'll be by this evening to see her."

"That's it! There's our in. *That's* the connection," Nathan exclaimed as he disconnected the call. "I feel it in my gut. Now. How do we prove it?"

"Maybe he works for the library system in some way," Rick said immediately. "But all four victims lived in different cities, so it stands to reason they would all have just gone to the branches closest to them, instead of all using the same one. And I just don't see someone rotating through working in every single branch throughout the county, do you? I don't even know if they do that. So, the most logical assumption is that he has access to their mainframe. Whether or not that access was obtained legitimately is another question."

"So how do we figure out who the killer is without tipping him off?" Hank asked.

The quartet fell silent, each pondering the question, until Lizzie gasped.

"What?" Nathan asked.

"Mary Adams. Annie told me once that her mom was a librarian for *years* up in Tulsa," Lizzie revealed. "I bet she could help us figure this out, or at least give us some insight."

"We won't be able to read her in on anything about our cases specifically, but yes, it's worth a shot to ask her some general questions," Nathan agreed. "Nothing to lose by trying."

Lizzie dialed Donny's number.

"Hey, babe. Have John and Mary gotten back from the hospital yet?"

"Not yet, but I expect them anytime now."

"Can you have her call me when they get there? It's important."

"Sure thing."

Lizzie hung up with a rueful smile.

"And now, I guess we wait."

"In the meantime, Hank, reach out to Gabe Crosson and see if any of our victims' names or the name Betty Mirelander are familiar to her."

"On it," Hank replied as he stood and stepped over to a corner of the room to make the call.

In mere moments he'd returned to his chair, shaking his head.

"Gabe doesn't know any of them."

Eighteen minutes later Lizzie's cell phone rang.

"Hello, Lizzie," Mary Adams said. "Donny said you needed to talk to me?"

"Yes, well, *we* do," Lizzie told her. "We've got some general questions about libraries and were hoping you could answer them."

"I can certainly try, dear."

"Great! Let me put you on speaker. Hang on just a moment."

Lizzie did that, then set her cell phone on the table.

"Hello, Ms. Adams. Nathan Thomas here."

"Why, hello there! How may I help you?"

"Well, ma'am, we have a bit of a quandary. We have a case involving libraries, and…"

"Let me guess. You need to know if there's any particularly optimal way to get data that pertains to your case."

"Something like that, yes."

"Well, see, here's the deal. Libraries greatly value and protect the privacy of their patrons. But all librarians are acutely aware that if a governmental agency has a search warrant and delivers it to the library, they *must* turn over their records," Mary began.

"Because of that, when you are looking up a *book* in the library's computer system, you will only ever be able to see data for the last two times it was checked out. By data, I mean patron name and other relevant info. You'd be able to see that it's been checked out ten thousand times, but only the names and details of the last two people to check it out will show up. And librarians only keep those two in there in case the book gets damaged or lost."

"Why is that, exactly?" Nathan asked.

"Honestly? Because it keeps law enforcement from being able to investigate people based solely on a book. If that practice wasn't in place, they conceivably could decide to target *everyone* who's ever checked out a certain title," she replied, then paused.

"Any questions?"

"None so far."

"Good. On the other hand," she continued, "if you have a warrant requesting records specifically by *patron name* rather than by book, you'd be able to see everything that individual has ever checked out. And just so you know - that approach *also* tends to be better received by library staff, because it lessens disruptions to our privacy policies. *That* would be the way I'd go about it if I were you."

"Thanks for the tip! I've only got one more question, if you don't mind."

"Not at all, go right ahead."

"How feasible would it be for a library employee to rotate through each of a large city or a county's public library locations?"

"In my experience, it wouldn't be," Mary replied immediately. "It wasn't that way up in Tulsa, anyway. Each of our branches had its own set budget and set number of assigned workers based on that branch's size and customer base, and those budgets were set annually by the city council. Volunteers, *maybe*, but *paid* staff? No. Because they were operating under very strict budget parameters."

"Thank you so much, Ms. Adams, you've been very helpful."

"Anytime, Agent Thomas," she replied cheerfully. "Anytime."

Lizzie hung up the call and smiled across the table at Nathan.

"Time to read in the Director?"

One of Rick's computers chiming delayed the answer.

"Sorry, let me just..." Rick's voice trailed off as he reviewed additional results of the last search commands he'd given.

"Seriously?"

"What is it?" Lizzie asked him.

"Betty Mirelander," he replied. "I'll give you three guesses where she worked for the last forty-four years."

"Yep, time to fill the Director in," Nathan agreed, and left the room.

Nathan returned several minutes later with the Director, who took the seat at the end of the table and said simply, "All right, lay it out for me."

They each took their turns familiarizing the big boss with the finer points of each case.

"Have the electronics yielded any evidence?" the Director asked, and everyone looked Rick's direction for those answers.

Rick dutifully summarized the IT portion to date, ending with, "The IP trace finally pinged back to an address in Lake Worth. The property owner died six weeks ago. However, she was a long-time employee at Tarrant County library, so my inclination is that the killer accessed the library's mainframe system from her house, possibly even using her login credentials in some manner to do so. But I can't prove my theory out until we get onsite."

The group quieted and waited as the Director reflected on everything he'd just heard.

"I agree that four warrants, one per victim name, is the way to proceed here," he said at length. "And it's probably best if you serve them separately, at different branches and different times, since we believe our primary suspect could be an employee. Less chance of tipping him off."

"Also, the Patriot Act is applicable here," the Director continued calmly. "Invoking that will enable us to access the library's background data logs as well, so that we can pinpoint *who* on their staff looked at our victims' patron profiles. Had our suspect not detonated explosives in a state-owned facility, we might not have that leverage. But his actions at the convention center fall under Patriot Act parameters."

He looked over at Nathan.

"Get warrant requests put together for Tarrant County Library – four victims, then a separate data log request. Without more definitive information, I don't believe the Lake Worth property search request will pass muster – *yet*. So, let's hope our interactions with the library yield enough useful evidence to be able to assist us in obtaining a search warrant for Betty Mirelander's residence."

"Get them to me as quickly as you can, and I'll get them expedited for you. Nice work so far, people. Keep it up," he said in closing, then stood, nodded his approval, and left.

Down the street, Bella's day had finally improved. When she returned from lunch, she'd found that her user access issues had completely disappeared.

Grateful, she'd immediately launched into the first project – a romance novel in English that she was translating into French. She'd been so absorbed in her work that five o'clock arrived without warning.

She saved and closed the files, logged out, and gathered up her purse.

Now for the drive home. This ought to be fun.

And when almost an hour passed and she wasn't even halfway home, she sighed and pressed the hands-free button on her steering wheel.

"Hey, Sarah," she said when her sister-in-law answered. "I don't think I'm going to make it back before the daycare closes. Can you pick Charlie up, please?"

"I figured it might be a little hectic for you," Sarah replied. "So, I went and got him around four this afternoon. I've already got dinner going, too. You just be careful and get home safe, and we'll see you soon!"

"You're the best, Sarah. Thanks."

Next, she called Nathan.

"Hey, honey," he said. "I've got maybe another hour here before I head home."

"Well, I'm only halfway there myself, unfortunately," she revealed. "Traffic is an absolute nightmare. But Charlie's taken care of. Sarah went and picked him up already."

"Good. Hey, I need to get back to this, but I will call you when I leave the office."

"You bet. Love you."

"Love you too, Bella, and I'm looking forward to hearing how the rest of your first day went when I get home."

Nathan hung up from taking his wife's call just in time to hear Rick mention, "You know, if we build out the first warrant request, then copy it and just use the 'find and replace' feature to sub out relevant fields for the other ones, this will go a *lot* faster."

"I like the way you think," Hank said. "Because the sooner we get *those* to the Director, the sooner *I* can go see how Annie is doing."

They implemented Rick's idea, and the team compiled all five warrant requests and sent them to the Director within a half-hour. Then they parted ways for the evening. Rick and Lizzie each headed straight home while Nathan and Hank both detoured first to Harris Hospital as promised.

When Hank arrived at the hospital, he was pleasantly surprised to find that Annie had indeed been moved out of the cardiac care unit.

He rode the elevator to the seventh floor, then followed the signs leading him to the south hallway and rooms seven-ten through seven-twenty-five. He was almost to her room when he saw John and Mary Adams come into view.

"Hello again, young man," John said, extending his hand. "They got her moved up here about two hours ago, and boy was she happy."

Hank chuckled.

"I bet. Are you guys leaving?"

"Yes," Mary confirmed. "John's taking me out to dinner. But we'll be back up here in the morning."

"You guys have fun," Hank said with a smile, and walked past them and toward Annie's room.

She noticed him standing in the doorway before he even had a chance to knock.

"Hi!" Annie exclaimed as she turned down the TV's volume. "I'm so happy to see you."

"Hi, honey," he replied as he leaned down to kiss her.

"I'm happy to see you too. You're in a pretty good mood."

"I am," she admitted. "Much better than this morning, at least. Sorry about that, by the way."

"No worries," he assured her as he sat on the edge of the bed and took her hand.

"So, tell me everything," she prompted. "Did any new evidence turn up? What did the lab results look like on that second bottle?"

"Oh, I see. Just gonna pump me for information, huh?" Hank teased.

"Absolutely. I am living vicariously through you since I am stuck in here, so, spill. I want *all* the details."

He laughed and pivoted to stretch out beside her.

"Well," he began, "I followed up on the rest of Sybil Planchet's background check, but nothing popped. I mean, *nothing*. So then we...".

As he continued to share all the day's developments and discoveries, Annie snuggled in close to him and hung on every word, occasionally asking him questions.

After a long while he noticed that she'd stopped asking questions, and he glanced down to see that Annie was sound asleep. Hank gently maneuvered himself off her bed, kissed her cheek, and headed home for dinner, a shower, and bed.

***

"Daddy! Hi!"

"Hey, buddy. Did you have a good day today?" Nathan asked as he scooped up Charlie and headed over to the coffee table to set his briefcase down.

"Yep! Aunt Sarah made s'ghetti. I put cheese on mine, and it was good. Want some?"

"I sure do. Come on, kiddo."

"Hey, sorry I'm late," Nathan said as he and Charlie walked into the kitchen where Bella and Sarah were seated at the table.

"I kept stuff warm, it's on the stove," Sarah pointed out. "Once you get your food come have a seat and we can update you."

"On?" he asked as he set Charlie down, then grabbed a plate and loaded it up.

"My retail space," she said proudly.

"And the rest of my first day," Bella added with a smile. "It got quite a bit better after lunch."

By the time Lizzie got home she was tired and hungry, and she grinned from ear to ear when she realized Donny had whipped up his famous carne asada and cheese enchiladas.

"That smells *amazing*," she proclaimed.

"Give it fifteen more minutes, it'll be ready," he answered. "So, you've got time to take a hot shower if you want, honey. And after dinner I'll rub your feet."

"That *sounds* amazing. You're batting a thousand right now, mister," Lizzie quipped with a smile before leaning into him for a kiss.

"You'll love this, then. John and Mary decided to make a trip back up to see Annie, then have dinner out," he shared. "It's just you and me, babe."

"I have to admit, I don't see how they do all this stuff all the time," Rick told Faith as they sat down to dinner. "I mean, being neck deep in tech again is cool and all, but I didn't realize just how much I signed on for."

"Are you thinking about changing your mind?"

"I am," he confirmed. "I'm beginning to think getting involved full-time like this wasn't a good idea. I like being helpful, don't get me wrong. But I opened the bookstore for a reason. And lately, I only set foot in it to pass straight through it to come upstairs."

He reached over and took her hand.

"Not to mention, I spent over half my Sunday away from you," he continued. "I've been there and done that and I am not sure I can be okay with a job taking over my life like that again. Before you and I met, it would have been fine. But not anymore."

"I'll support whatever you decide to do, you know that," Faith told him earnestly. "But you do need to decide soon, and if you opt to change your mind, you need to let Nathan know as soon as possible. He'll understand, hon."

Rick sighed.

"I know. And I will talk to him about it– *after* the cases we're working on right now are over."

Chapter Twenty-Three

True to his word, the Director expedited the process. By eight o'clock on Tuesday morning when the team returned, all five warrants had been signed off on by a judge and were ready to go.

They assembled in the conference room and Nathan quickly passed out the paperwork.

"We're going to stick with our original assignments. That means Lizzie, you've got Winger, Hank serves the warrant regarding Planchett, and I am on point to get Diane's records. Rick, I want you to travel to the main library downtown to handle both the Philips *and* the data log warrants, since you'll know best what we need from the mainframe. Whenever possible, I want each of you to deal with the branch manager directly, and if any of you see our suspect, call for backup and wait for them to arrive before you engage. We'll meet back here."

With that, the team dispersed, all of them focused on the task at hand - and one of them also wrestling with a weighty decision.

Lizzie pulled into the Grapevine, Texas branch's parking lot a little after nine a.m. and took a moment to make sure her papers were in order before she turned off her car and walked inside.

The young woman behind the circulation desk visibly paled at seeing the service weapon holstered at Lizzie's right hip.

"Good morning, miss. My name is Elizabeth Zimmerman, and I'm an agent with the Federal Bureau of Investigation. May I speak with your branch manager, please?"

Lizzie showed the woman her badge.

"Um, sure, ma'am. I'll get her. One moment, please," the library employee stammered, then fled to parts unknown.

Several minutes later a short, slender brunette woman approached.

"Agent Zimmerman, it's nice to meet you. Right this way, please."

Down in the Benbrook branch, the reaction to Hank's arrival was not quite as nervous, mainly because while he too was carrying a firearm, his holster was tucked against the small of his back underneath his jacket.

He introduced himself and showed the attendant the temporary FBI credentials that the Director had provided, then smiled and nodded when asked to wait just a moment while the branch manager was located.

Nathan's arrival time at the Keller branch was sooner than he'd expected; he'd figured that traffic would be heavier than it turned out to be. Taking it as a good omen, he ventured inside, showed his credentials, and asked to speak to the individual in charge.

The manager's reaction to his presence surprised him.

"Agent... Thomas, is it?" she asked as she peered through her bifocals at his identification card, and then blinked up at him.

From Nathan's best estimation, she was around five feet two inches tall at the most, with plump cheeks, closely cropped silver hair, and a slightly befuddled expression.

"Yes, ma'am. Could we speak privately?"

She clapped her hands together with glee and behind her glasses he could plainly see her blue eyes take on a sparkle.

"It's about a *murder*, isn't it?" she stage-whispered in a paper-thin voice that was trembling with utter excitement. "I do *love* a good murder mystery! Right this way."

He only barely managed to keep from smiling as he followed her to her office.

Rick's trip to the main branch of the Tarrant County library system was anticlimactic by comparison. The branch manager, an older gentleman who in Rick's opinion looked perpetually bored, happened to be the one manning the circulation desk.

Upon hearing Rick's request, he held out his hand for the paperwork, scanned both warrants' contents, then said blandly, "I'll have this for you shortly. Wait here."

Rick had a printout of everything he needed and was returning to his vehicle within a half-hour.

By ten-thirty they'd gathered around the conference room table once more.

"Okay, let's see what we have," Nathan prompted, and the review of data began. The room fell eerily silent, each of them skimming reports.

Lizzie was the first to comment.

"Demetrious Winger checked out the newest Gabe Crosson series three weeks ago," she said. "All five books."

"Which books are those?" Nathan asked her.

"It's her *Joe Broken, P.I.* books – *Broken Trust, Broken Bones, Broken Lives, Broken Dreams,* and *Broken Hearts.*"

Hank skimmed Sybil Planchett's check-out history.

"Sybil did too, back in March."

"Sugar read them all in February," Rick chimed in.

They all looked at Nathan and waited as he reviewed Diane Mackinaw's borrower history.

"She checked out the first one on April third, and the fifth one just last week."

Meanwhile, Rick skimmed the pages of his data log retrieval, paused, and grabbed a highlighter from the small collection of them that were sitting toward the middle of the table.

He made one mark, then another, then another, flipping pages rapidly.

"Guys," he began, "you really aren't gonna believe this."

"Go for it," Nathan prompted.

"Okay. Betty Mirelander died six weeks ago, right?" Rick said evenly. "But check this out. Her username is showing up as having reviewed all four of our victims' accounts within the last month. And that's not all. Our killer also accessed *nine others.*"

He looked over at Nathan.

"He targeted nine other people, Nathan. *Please* tell me that we finally have enough for that freaking search warrant."

"I believe we just might. Liz, can you ask the Director to join us, please?"

"Sure. Be right back."

The Director's eyebrows shot skyward as he was brought up to speed.

"*Now* we have enough concrete evidence to proceed with a

search warrant for the Lake Worth location," he informed them. "And make damn sure that the wording allows for lawful detainment of anyone on the property in question."

"On it, sir. You'll have it in your inbox within the hour," Nathan assured him.

Once the Director had left the room, Nathan redirected his attention to Lizzie, Hank, and Rick.

"Split up those nine names between you and start doing welfare checks," he instructed. "Hopefully our suspect hasn't gotten to any of them yet. Find them and arrange to get them transported here as soon as possible. Get local police involved as needed."

With that, Nathan returned to his office to build a very carefully worded search warrant request for Betty Mirelander's legal address of record.

"Okay," Hank said, clapping his hands together. "Let's divvy these up by address maybe?"

Rick skimmed down the pages.

"We've got one in Arlington, one in Euless...".

"Pardon me, but - we ought to start with a quick cross-check of these names against recent obituaries and homicides in the area," Lizzie interrupted, her tone neutral. "Hell, it'd be even faster to just call the Tarrant County coroner's office and ask Jerry Broder if he's had any of them come across his autopsy table. My point is, confirm the worst first, and *then* get moving to save whoever is left."

"You don't think we'll get lucky enough to save all nine of them," Rick observed. "I can tell by your expression."

Lizzie caught and held his gaze.

"Honestly?"

"Of course."

"I wish I could tell you that I believe we'll save them all, Rick. I really do. But I've just seen way too much in my career," she said sadly.

"The things they all had in common were as random and obscure as owning a library card and reading a certain author's books. The likelihood of that connection being made in a typical police investigation is very small. Not to mention, take a minute and think about just how close together the five events we already know about happened. Within a week, maybe ten days, tops? Now, compare that against the fact that our suspect targeted these people *weeks* ago - and that until very recently, he was flying completely below anyone's radar. I mean, if Jerry Broder hadn't reached out to Nathan about Sybil Planchett's strange autopsy results, he still might be. I hate to say it, but my gut says we *might* find one or two still alive. Maybe three, if we're lucky."

She took a deep breath then exhaled slowly.

"I really hope I'm wrong here. But I don't think I am. So, let's get Broder on speakerphone and get this part over with."

Within ten minutes they had their confirmation, and Lizzie's soul ached with the knowledge that unfortunately, her assessment had been spot on.

Of the nine names relayed to the coroner, he verified performing autopsies on seven of them - including Hollie Blumfeld and Ming Castlebrook - in the past few weeks.

"Thanks, Dr. Broder," she said glumly, and disconnected the call.

"Okay," she sighed. "Let's go update Nathan, and then try to save the two that we still can. Where do they live?"

It was almost three p.m. by the time the two remaining – and completely oblivious - targets were located and safely tucked away in the smaller conference room on the eighth floor.

By three-thirty an express courier had hand-delivered the finalized search warrant for Betty Mirelander's home.

The ten-person raid team, led by Nathan, climbed into two black SUVs and left the Dallas office's parking garage at a quarter to five.

Nathan had opted to add Grace Womack and Herb Davis in on the assignment, then rounded out his crew with four other seasoned agents. After briefing everyone, Nathan was leading the walk to the elevator when he was pulled aside by the Director, which had delayed their departure time by ten precious minutes.

Traffic was already starting to fill in heavily in and around the downtown area by the time the team got underway, causing Nathan to swear under his breath.

"Lake Worth PD is meeting us where, exactly?"

"Their SWAT team is meeting us about a mile from the residence," Hank told him, and because Hank just couldn't help himself, he quickly added, "*If* we can ever get out of the Dallas city limits, that is."

The snarky comment had the desired effect of turning the corners of Nathan's mouth upward, if only temporarily.

"Let's go over the lay of the land again," he said to Lizzie.

"Three-bedroom two-bath brick one-story home on a corner lot. The floor plan is straightforward. Basically, a big rectangular box," she replied, and handed him the schematic. "The front door feeds right into the living room and open kitchen areas. As you move down the hallway there are two bedrooms with a bathroom between them on the left side and the master suite is further down on the right. The back door's right in line with the front door."

"Okay, Hank, you and Grace will be leading a team of three around to the back. We'll have one team member each watching the north and south sides of the house respectively in case someone tries to exit through a window. We're going to use a battering ram on the front door, but I'm thinking a quieter entrance through the back door unless we don't have any other choice."

"Agreed. And often, the back door locks aren't as robust, so they're easier to pick," Hank agreed. "It would be better to keep our entry from that direction subtle if we can."

"Who's on point for the front door team?" Lizzie asked.

"Me, Herb, and two SWAT guys," Nathan replied, a little too casually. "I want you and Rick coming in once the house is secured."

I understand why Rick is hanging back at first. He's tech, not muscle, so we need him to hack any security systems onsite, and then run diagnostics once we're in. But I've always *been on point before,* Lizzie thought to herself, then crinkled her nose in frustration.

She turned her head to look at Grace, eyebrows raised as if to say, 'did you hear that crap just now?'

The knowing glance and small nod Grace gave her confirmed that Grace had noticed the abrupt departure from the norm, too.

With nothing much left to discuss, the team in the lead SUV settled into a tense, uneasy silence.

An hour later the twin SUVs were rolling to a stop in an oversized parking lot. Nathan immediately hopped out and made his way over to a Lake Worth SWAT officer with sergeant insignia on both his sleeves.

After Nathan conferred with his Lake Worth counterpart, he returned to the vehicle's front passenger seat.

"Nathan, we just caught a break. I finally got a hit on facial recognition," Rick said, and showed him the alert he'd received on his phone.

"Everybody out," Nathan directed, "so Rick can update everybody at the same time before we get onsite."

Both teams converged between the two SUVs.

"Our suspect has been tentatively identified through facial recognition," Nathan announced, then gestured to Rick.

"Our guy's name is Angus Schultz, aged forty-six, six feet two-and-a-half inches tall and two hundred pounds. He popped up in Kansas Department of Revenue's database with an expired driver's license as of his birthday in January last year."

A few more last-minute preparation points, and the combined fourteen-member warrant team resumed their travel to the house in question.

But none of them could have foreseen the outcome.

Nathan's breach team assembled as planned and approached the front door, a SWAT member holding the battering ram and standing out of sight of the peephole, while Hank's team stealthily made their way around the side and to the back of the home.

Hearing 'in position' in his earpiece, Nathan reached forward to knock on the door. To his surprise, it swung open, and as he backed away a few steps and hurriedly drew his weapon, he found himself face-to-face with a calm and smiling Angus Schultz.

"Good evening! Can I help you?"

"We're looking for Angus," Nathan stated.

"I'm so sorry, I don't know who that is," the man answered, and then extended his hand to Nathan.

"I apologize, I seem to have forgotten my manners. Hi, I'm Gabe Crosson. It's very nice to meet you. Would you like to come in?"

Angus Schultz was taken into custody without incident. Once he had been handcuffed and handed over to Lake Worth PD for transport, it was time to collect evidence. Rick immediately situated himself in front of the sleek collection of electronic gadgetry, flexed his gloved fingers with glee, and set about exploring Schultz's system. The rest of the FBI team went to work searching for evidence throughout the remainder of the house.

"What the *hell*," Lizzie breathed forty minutes later.

She was in the master bedroom closet gathering evidence and had found a small, ornately carved wooden box that had been buried under a mountain of clothes. The box was eight inches long, four inches wide, and four inches deep. She photographed it from multiple angles, then reached out with a gloved right hand to flick open the tiny latch that was holding it closed.

Inside she found several items, including a small paperweight with obvious blood spatter on it, a bottle of red clover supplements, a charm bracelet, a college ring, a bottle of nail polish, and a necklace that looked awfully familiar.

"Nathan," she called out, and snapped several pictures of the contents while she waited for him.

"What have you got?" he asked when he appeared in the narrow doorway.

She grasped both ends of the broken silver chain and lifted it slowly from the box.

"Diane's necklace."

"Yep."

"Bag it and mark it priority," he instructed, and she nodded and carefully returned the necklace to its resting place before closing the lid and sliding the entire box into a thick, clear plastic evidence bag.

Chapter Twenty-Four

"It's mind blowing," Rick commented the next morning as he and the others gathered in the conference room.

An hour into the evidence collection process, Nathan had received word that Angus Schultz had become belligerent and combative during transport, injuring himself and a SWAT team member in the process. Standard policy dictated that he first be treated for his injuries.

Angus had been transported first to Harris Hospital for medical treatment, and then to the Tarrant County jail to await placement in a state-run psychiatric unit for evaluation at the request of the public defender assigned to him.

As a result, the impetus was on Nathan and his team to try to piece their case together via other means, since their usual avenue of questioning the suspect had been temporarily blocked.

But Rick had stayed up well into the wee hours of the morning and had uncovered most of the background on Angus Schultz. He was prepared to walk them all through it once the Director arrived.

At last, the Director came into the conference room, shutting the door behind him.

"Apologies, I was tied up on a call," he announced as he took his seat.

"Rick," Nathan said simply, and nodded once.

"The summarized version is, Angus Schultz is the illegitimate child of Betty Mirelander," Rick began. "In digging through hers and Schultz's backgrounds, it came to light that Betty got pregnant in 1970 when she was sixteen and was sent to live with her aunt in Kansas. She gave the baby up for adoption and returned to her parents' home in Lake Worth."

"Angus grew up in a small farm town in Kansas called Lecompton. Parts of his records were sealed through a juvenile court, but evidently his adoptive parents gave up on him at some point. He spent a lot of years in and out of foster care before he aged out of the system."

"I went through his computer with a fine-toothed comb and was able to pinpoint the exact timeframe that he searched out his birth mother and figured out her location. That was in November of last year."

"So, he found her and came to visit," Lizzie mused. "That makes sense. But it doesn't explain what the hell set him off."

"Well, among other things, he was diagnosed with paranoid schizophrenia at the age of nineteen," Rick answered. "And from my research, I think I know what might have prompted him specifically to become violent. Generally, most people suffering from schizophrenia aren't."

"What did you find?" Hank asked.

"Correspondence directed toward the real Gabe Crosson, going back three years," came the answer. "Angus started off as a fan and newsletter club member, but over the last six months or so the tone of the messages moved from typical fan interaction to more foreboding and then downright threatening."

He paused.

"It's actually the last two messages to her that he drafted, but never sent, that I think are the most relevant here," Rick continued, and gestured toward the drop-down screen where he was now displaying the first unsent email in question.

"Take a look for yourselves. Here's the first one, dated about eight weeks ago."

He waited a minute or two while the others in the group scanned the big screen's contents.

"And, here's the last one, dated the day that Betty Mirelander died," Rick prompted, as he clicked a button to show the second, most graphic email.

"*Wow*," Nathan said as his eyes skimmed the hate-filled rant.

"Yeah. By the time he wrote this last one, he was firmly convinced that *he* was the real Gabe Crosson, and that the actual Gabe was nothing but a thief and a liar. As you can see, he was *very* specific - and graphic - about what needed to happen to her, as well as to anyone who read her work or supported her in any way, including Betty. It's clear from this last email that Angus truly believed his birth mother was stealing stories from his mind as he slept and giving them to Gabe Crosson to publish."

Nathan glanced over at the Director.

"We need to pull Betty Mirelander's autopsy results and case file," he suggested. "Her death might not have been natural after all."

"Agreed," the Director said.

"So, did he actually use Betty's login to access the system, or did he hack it? Lizzie asked, and Rick nodded.

"Both. I found evidence that he hacked into the library's system – but only long enough to restore her username to active status. They would have archived it once they'd heard she died. He simply turned it back on, then logged in as her for the subsequent searches he made. Which in my opinion underscores where he was mentally at the time. It would have been much cleaner, not to mention harder to trace, if he'd just done his searches when he broke in. But by repeatedly using her info, he left an obvious breadcrumb trail."

Friday morning revealed a very happy Annie Adams leaving behind a hospital gown for a pair of sweats and an oversized t-shirt of Hank's – the clothes she'd worn to the book fair had been cut away from her body in the emergency room.

The nurse settled her into a wheelchair and smoothly rolled her down the hall to the elevator, having sent Hank on ahead to retrieve his truck and drive it to the designated patient pick-up area.

Before long, Annie found herself squinting in bright sunlight as they continued outside and over to where Hank waited.

He helped her step up into the truck and she carefully lowered herself into Hank's passenger seat, then waved goodbye to the nurse.

"You all right?" he asked after he reached in and fastened her seat belt for her.

"I'm fine, Hank, I promise," she told him. "I'm still a little sore, and everything still sounds like it's underwater in my right ear, but otherwise, I'm great. You know I am, or they wouldn't be sending me home."

Hank leaned in and kissed her.

"I know, baby," he told her. "And I'm so glad you're okay. What do you say we get out of here?"

"Music to my ears."

He closed her door, went around to the other side of the truck and climbed behind the wheel.

"Hey, now that you're out," he said as he put the transmission into drive, "you wanna go with me to Nathan and Bella's on Memorial Day?"

Annie reached over and took his hand.

"I'd love to."

Nathan and Lizzie were summoned to the sixth-floor lab to review test results on the wooden box's contents at around two-thirty Friday afternoon.

"The paperweight had Demetrious Winger's blood on it, and the shape of its base perfectly matches the void in the bloodstain patterns in the evidence photos," the tech began. "That red clover bottle had Sybil Planchett's prints all over it. The nail polish bottle had fingerprints on it that matched up to Ming Castlebrook. And the necklace? Diane Mackinaw's."

"What about the college ring, charm bracelet, and the other five items?" Lizzie asked.

"I'm sorry, there wasn't any usable trace on them, so there's just no way for me to confirm who they belong to. You'll probably have to reach out to the remaining victims' family members to help with that part."

"What about the box itself?" Nathan asked.

"Angus Schultz's prints, and only his prints, were all over it."

At four p.m. that Friday afternoon Rick stood in Nathan's office doorway and rapped on the frame.

"You got a minute?"

"Sure, come on in. Just finishing up an email right quick," Nathan answered, and continued typing for a few moments, then pressed 'enter'.

"And..... *done*," he said. "Whatcha got?"

Rick stepped into the room, closed the door behind him, and sat in one of Nathan's visitor chairs.

"Uh oh," Nathan said. "You don't look happy. What's going on?"

"I changed my mind," Rick said bluntly. "I thought I knew what I was getting myself into when I said yes to coming aboard full-time. But this is quickly overtaking everything, including time with my wife, and I am not okay with that."

He leaned forward.

"After my first wife and my kids died, I lived and breathed the job because it was all I had left. And looking back, I was miserable. It kept me alive, but I was miserable. I won't ever go back to that, Nathan. *Ever*."

Nathan tilted his head and looked at his brother-in-law for a long moment.

"I understand," he finally said.

"You do?"

"One hundred percent," Nathan confirmed. "To be honest, I was amazed you ever said yes in the first place."

"Okay. *Not* the reaction I was expecting, I'll be honest," Rick said with a chuckle.

"This isn't for everyone," Nathan said simply. "And yeah, it will take over your life if you're not careful. So, I totally get it, and we're good. All right?"

"Just for the record, you do know you can still call me when you need an occasional consult, right? I'm not saying 'never ever again', just, not full time."

"Yep, we will just go back to the way it was."

"Cool, thanks."

"You and Faith still coming over on Monday?"

"Wouldn't miss it. Noon, right?"

"Yep, see you then."

Memorial Day arrived with almost perfect temperatures for an outdoor gathering in North Texas. Nathan nursed a beer and manned the grill while Bella acted as both the hostess to their guests and the liaison between him and Sarah, who'd taken over the kitchen to make tasty homemade side dishes and desserts.

At one point Lizzie found herself standing side-by-side with Nathan, and the grudge she'd carried since the Lake Worth warrant finally bubbled up and out into the open.

"Why did you bench me?" she asked and threw him completely off guard.

"When?"

"Lake Worth, and don't pretend you don't know what I'm talking about," she retorted, crossing her arms over her chest.

He sighed.

"Look, Liz, I had no idea what we might have been walking into out there, and yeah, I opted to be overly cautious."

She started to protest but his next words deflated her anger.

"You're my family. You know that, right? At least, I hope you do. And because of that, I worry about you anyway, but now I *really* worry, because you're carrying my niece or nephew. So, yeah, I changed the lineup. I didn't bench you, I just... moved you further down in the batting order, is all. Just until I knew that everything was clear."

"Do me a favor and just give me a heads up beforehand next time, okay?"

Now he was surprised.

"You're not pissed?"

She shrugged.

"I was, but I am also realizing that I need to adjust my approach. I'm so used to being on the job and throwing myself into whatever happens without a second thought, you know? So, it honestly didn't even occur to me that taking point on barging in on a homicidal maniac wouldn't exactly be the safest thing to do."

He leaned over and murmured, "Don't let Donny hear you say that, or he will try to talk you into just staying home until that kid's born."

She laughed.

"He'd try, at least. Jury's out on whether he'd succeed."

Nathan looked her in the eyes.

"You and I. Are we good?"

Lizzie smiled.

"Yeah, boss. We're good. Thanks for watching out for me."

Hank and Annie's arrival caused a raucous cheer in the backyard, and while he went to get her a drink, Annie was gently hugged by everyone in attendance.

"It's great to see you," Lizzie said sincerely.

"Thanks. Grateful to still be here, for sure. And I hope to be able to come back to work next week."

"You sure you'll be ready?"

"Hey, you of all people do not get to judge me," Annie fired back with a grin. "We had to write stuff down for you for two weeks and you insisted on pushing through it and working anyway."

Lizzie laughed out loud before she carefully draped her arm around Annie's shoulders.

"Touché. So, you and Hank... you happy?"

Annie beamed.

"Like you wouldn't believe."

"Good. I'm happy for you, Annie. Truly."

When the doorbell rang a third time, Sarah Thomas frowned. Everyone was out in the backyard but her, and with the music playing out there she was certain that none of them could hear much else.

I thought everyone had arrived already...

She quickly dusted the flour off her hands as best she could before she hustled to the door and swung it open.

"Hey, sorry I'm..." a rich tenor voice started to say, then trailed off.

Sarah stared at the stranger on the front porch, temporarily struck mute by his brown eyes, thick black hair, and the way he was gazing at her.

"I'm sorry, I must have the wrong house," he said, a puzzled expression on his face.

"Who are you looking for?" she asked, then flinched as he stretched out his hand toward her face.

He widened his eyes at her, withdrew his hand, and smiled sheepishly.

"Sorry. Force of habit. You've just got... you've got a little flour on your face."

Sarah's cheeks flushed beet red.

"Oh," she managed self-consciously. "Hazard of the trade, I guess.... who were you looking for again?"

"Nathan Thomas. He invited me to a party?"

"You've got the right place, then. Come on in."

His smile widened, and her breath caught a little.

"Thanks," he said, and stepped inside.

"Where should I put this?" he asked and held up a twelve-pack of beer.

"Follow me, we'll make room in the fridge."

They retreated to the kitchen, and he looked around approvingly.

"You bake. Nice! And that explains the flour," he teased, his eyes sparkling with mirth. "I like cooking, myself."

"Thanks," Sarah said. "Like I said, hazards of the trade."

She moved to the counter to grab a paper towel and wipe off her face.

"So, how do you know Nathan?"

"I know him and Lizzie both," he replied as he placed the beer in the fridge, then grabbed himself one, and shut the door. "I used to be an agent."

He held out his hand.

"Name's Jones. Tristan Jones."

"Hello there, Tristan Jones," she said as she clasped his warm, strong hand in hers. "Nice to meet you. I'm Sarah, Nathan's sister."

"Beautiful name," he said softly before he let go of her hand and cleared his throat.

"So, what are you making?"

"Lemon bars," she answered.

"Get out. Really? I love lemon bars, and I'd like to learn how to make them," he told her.

"Seriously?"

"Seriously. Did you not hear me say earlier that I like to cook, too? I can throw down some mean dinners – just ask Lizzie and Donny, they'll tell you. But I don't know how to make many desserts. So, can I help?"

"You sure you wouldn't rather go mingle?" she asked and gestured toward the back reaches of the house.

He shook his head slowly, his eyes never breaking contact with hers.

"Something tells me that the most interesting person here at this party is in the kitchen," he said solemnly, and made her smile.

"Well, then," she murmured, "I guess we'd better get started."

Epilogue

OVER THE COURSE of the following weeks Hollie Blumfeld's mother confirmed the college ring belonged to her only child, and Sugar Philip's aunt flew in from Memphis to verify that the charm bracelet found was Sugar's. The remaining five victims' families followed suit.

Betty Mirelander's remains were exhumed for extensive forensic testing. It would later be determined that her actual cause of death mirrored that of Sybil Rose Planchett's.

Five weeks after being attacked, lone survivor Diane Mackinaw returned to work as the Dallas FBI office's unit secretary, using a stylish hand-carved cane to assist her movements. While her doctors felt confident in saying that she might very well walk unaided again someday, the raspy overtone in her voice caused by her injuries was unfortunately permanent.

After a twenty-four-month wait, Angus Schultz was finally examined and found to be mentally unfit to stand trial. He was transported to North Texas State Hospital in Vernon, Texas, the state's only maximum-security mental health facility, where he was institutionalized for the remainder of his days.

Somewhere along the way the press corps, having somehow gotten wind of some of the details of the case, dubbed Angus Schultz "The Dewey Decimal Killer" due to his chosen method of selecting his victims.

Author's Note

Just FYI - there IS no "Tarrant County library"; in the North Texas area, as I imagine is the case in other places, each town maintains its own independent library system. But having all this mayhem confined to a single set of city limits just wouldn't have been nearly as much fun! So, I opted to employ a little poetic license to tell this story.

Special thanks to former librarian Havila Workman, who schooled me well regarding life on the other side of the library counter – and who didn't roll her eyes *too* hard at me when I took some existing suppositions of mine and just ran with them because it made the story more exciting!

Join my *spam-free* newsletter to stay updated on the latest news and events!

SUBSCRIBE

Author's Note

Follow me on Facebook
Follow me on BookBub
Follow me on Goodreads

Also by D.F. Hart

Vital Secrets

Mystery, Suspense and Thriller written as D.F. Hart

Wall of Secrets (prequel)

Book of Secrets

List of Secrets

Web of Secrets

Path of Secrets

Carnival of Secrets

House of Secrets

End of Secrets

Return of Secrets

Vital Secrets, Volume 1-3

Vital Secrets, Volume 4-6

COMING SOON (2024 - 2026)

Game of Secrets

Network of Secrets

War of Secrets

Raven's Path - Coming in 2024

Mystery, Suspense and Thriller written as D.F. Hart

Raven's Rise

Raven's Attack

One Last Gift – An Anthology by James N. Richardson (D.F. Hart, Editor & Publisher)

Love's Defender Series

Steamy romantic suspense

Saving Brielle

Minding Mari

Protecting Andria

Another Try Novellas

Contemporary romance

Never Say Sorry

Save Me a Dance

Falling into Place

Love Notes

Read My Lips

Out of the Blue

One Last Try

The Another Try Collection

About the Author

D.F. Hart resides in Texas. Her favorite authors include Frederick Forsyth, Ken Follet, and J.D. Robb. Other interests include hidden object and puzzle games -she loves a good mystery storyline!

Of writing, she says: "It's a lot of work, but also an escape. A lot of tears and sweat go into a story, building believable characters, shaping the plot so that the reader can't wait to turn the page. Sometimes I'll wake up at 3 a.m. with that perfect line that escaped me earlier in the day running through my head. But it's worth it. And the brilliant part is, you get to create a little universe of your own. Anything can happen; there are no limits."

She happily pens mysteries and thrillers under D.F. Hart, and contemporary and suspenseful romance as Faith Hart.

www.ingramcontent.com/pod-product-compliance
Lightning Source LLC
Chambersburg PA
CBHW030745190726
48285CB00003B/711